The Caduceus

*A Water
Chronicle
featuring
Dr. Francis
Allenton*

by Dennis Edwards

Plain View Press
P. O. 42255
Austin, TX 78704

plainviewpress.net
sbright1@austin.rr.com
1-512-441-2452

Cover Art: "Spirit of the Caduceus," Amanda Rae Edwards
MandyLady@aol.com

Art on title page: "Caduceus," J.D. Harris, Harris' Art Garden and Gallery,
Eureka Springs, AK
harrisartineureka@yahoo.com

Acknowledgments

I wish to acknowledge a number of people who have played instrumental roles in the creation of *The Caduceus*. I first thank my wife and in-house editor, Pamela, whose love is a light in a world gone mad. She is a solid judge of fiction and the person from whom the best attributes of my characters take form. I am grateful to my Mom, Betty, who has given encouragement and support to me in many ways and who in her own quest for happiness has overcome many obstacles. I deeply appreciate Plain View Press publisher and editor Susan Bright who saw merit in the tale and gently guided my efforts. I derived great joy from my daughter, Amanda, who overcame a time of personal difficulties to design the cover art for this book. I was blessed to meet J.D. and Cathy Harris, artists in Eureka Springs, Arkansas. Each day I enjoy the copper Caduceus that J.D. created following our discussion of this book. I thank family, friends and professionals who reviewed the manuscript and helped with accuracy and authenticity: Larry Smallie, Jim Walker, Rose Keene, Judy Halbert, Lou Turner, Jory Sherman, and Ty Doverspike. Last, I honor all who continue to fight for clean water and respond to the cries of those denied access to this basic, life-sustaining substance. To this cause I pledge a portion of the proceeds of this book.

Numbers 21:8 "And the Lord said unto Moses, Make thee a fiery serpent, and set it upon a pole and it shall come to pass, that everyone that is bitten, when he looketh upon it, shall live."

Chapter 1

"Is this the artifact?" Francis Allenton approached the Caduceus. Two brass serpents wound their way around a marble column. The brass had the look of antiquity.

"Surely as I live and die, this item came from the very tomb of Aesclepius. It has been in my personal family for generations, guarded and protected as a gift from the gods." The shopkeeper lied.

"The Staff of Aesclepius, right here in your shop?" Francis toyed with the man.

He had been coming to Greece for seven years. Each year as the spring semester wound down, Francis, a professor and researcher, made his arrangements to fly to Greece where he usually joined an archeological dig. He was a water scientist, but in truth, he was a driven man, obsessed by the Caduceus.

Francis had begun his search for an ancient Caduceus in Pompeii. On his first trip to Greece, a side visit to Pompeii was included in the travel package. While strolling one of Pompeii's streets, he had entered the shop of a physician and on the wall a beautifully preserved mural depicted a Caduceus. A vessel of water was being poured into the mouth of a brass snake, and from its tail, a cup was collecting the water.

From that time forward Francis was convinced that the Caduceus was not simply a symbol of healing, but an actual healing device. He had immersed himself in the myths of the Caduceus and the historical accounts of how it had emerged as a symbol of healing including its predecessor symbol, the Staff of Aesclepius.

The shopkeeper broke into his thoughts as he stood in front of the obvious fake.

"Are you interested in purchasing this splendid example of – "

"Not very." Francis quickly responded. "It is a beautiful piece of craftsmanship, but not as old as my mother."

"You insult me, sir." The shopkeeper kept his charade lively.

"As a copy, it intrigues me." Francis ran his fingers along the sensuous lines of the snakes as they intertwined. "What are you asking?"

"Eight hundred American dollars."

"For the original staff of Aesclepius?" Francis once again toyed with the shopkeeper.

"It is obvious, sir, that you are a specialist in artifacts and I, a simple shopkeeper, have been deluded by those who brought this artifact to me, representing it as an antiquity. My stupidity will cost me. As a reproduction I would be lucky to get my money back from it."

"Can you put me in touch with the artisans that brought this to you? I am interested in how they came to make it. I like to know these kinds of things. Say, for a hundred dollars American?"

"You are not interested in buying this beautiful and artistically rendered example?"

"Not really. But I would pay you a hundred dollars to meet the artist."

Francis' friend and university colleague traveling with him came into the shop.

"Are you done yet?" Mark asked.

"Just nearly."

Mark walked over to the counter.

"Not another Caduceus! When are you going to give this obsession of yours a rest?"

"When I find a real one." Francis replied. He turned back to the shop keeper. "Do we have a deal?"

"How about nine hundred for the Caduceus and the names?"

"Four!"

"Six."

"Five."

"Five and a half?"

"Done. Half now, and half when I meet them. I will leave the Caduceus in your care and keeping."

"You are a generous man. The men I am sending you to meet, they won't have any trouble from you?"

"No trouble from me. I just want to ask them some questions."

The shopkeeper called a young boy from the street. He spoke to him in Greek.

"This boy will take you." A boy with dark eyes smiled broadly at them. The shopkeeper gave the boy a small coin. Francis paid the shopkeeper, took a receipt and motioned for the boy to start. The boy skipped and walked down twisted streets. He was hard to follow.

"What's with this Caduceus search of yours?" Mark asked. "You're a water scientist. What's an ancient symbol got to do with your field of study?"

"What do you know about the Caduceus?" Francis asked.

"Universal symbol of medicine, isn't it?"

"Do you know of Aesclepius?"

"Not really."

The boy had slowed slightly as they began to climb a hill lined by white washed plaster walls.

"Aesclepius, I am convinced, was a real man. Not a myth, but a man, like you and me. He was deified as the god of medicine and the man and the myth became entwined. The Staff of Aesclepius was a single wooden staff around which a single serpent clung. A Sumerian vase from about 2000B.C. was found that depicted a single serpent staff."

"So, that's how you knew the one in the store was a fake. It had two serpents."

"Yes, and the staff was made of marble or some stone to simulate marble. The original staff of Aesclepius made of wood would long ago have disintegrated.

Aesclepius was probably a skilled physician in Greece around 1200 B.C. Medical schools developed by devotes to Aesclepius were called Aesclepions, temples of healing. Patients believed they could be healed simply by sleeping within the temples. The worship of Aesclepius spread to Rome and his methods of healing lasted as late as the sixth century. Fathers taught sons the healing arts. Harmless snakes were found in the Aesclepions, more as a tribute to Aesclepius than for any healing properties they may have had."

"I thought he was some kind of god, didn't you say that?"

"That is where the myths confound reality. Aesclepius was the son of Apollo and Coronis. Coronis, however, Apollo learned, had taken a mortal lover. The gods were ordered to kill Coronis and while she was burning on her funeral pyre Apollo felt pity for her and rescued her unborn child. The child, Aesclepius, was raised by a wise centaur who taught him how to heal. In one story Aesclepius brought a patient back from death."

"So, he was a central figure in ancient medicine."

"Yes, Aesclepius was such a central figure that the Hippocratic Oath was sworn to him and his children until a modern version was authored in the twentieth century."

"So, the Caduceus is homage to Aesclepius?"

"Well, yes and no. The Caduceus usually with two snakes on the pole topped by an omphalos stone didn't emerge until Roman times."

The young boy had stopped outside a small door. He gestured for the men to catch up. Francis gave him a small coin and walked through the door. The smell of fumes from a forge emerged as the men looked up from their work. A man approached who spoke no English. After gesturing angrily for Francis and Mark to leave, the man turned around as a young man entered the room behind him.

"May I help you?" the young man asked in broken English.

"I have purchased one of your splendid sculptures. At my request, I have been brought here to meet the artist. I am a collector of Caduceus related art."

The first man approached and an angry exchange took place between the two men. The younger man had an air of authority and calmed the situation.

"I am the artist," he proclaimed.

"How did you determine the form of the sculpture?" Francis asked.

"From an artifact."

"May I see it?"

"Follow me." The young man led them into the interior of the shop. Lifting a wooden box he removed a small woolen blanket. Inside the blanket was a brass snake wound around a decaying olive wood staff. The age of the brass was unmistakably ancient. The snake was flattened as if a large stone had fallen on it. It was still possible to determine that the snake was hollow, the mouth of the snake was exaggerated in an open position and the tail had a small opening.

"Where was this found?"

"I cannot say," the young man said. "It has been in my family for generations. My family has a long history of being healers. This was among the many things they passed down to me. I do not know the origin of this piece, but I know it is Greek and I know it comes from the ancient times."

"May I touch it?" Francis showed such genuine admiration the man allowed him to hold the piece. After examining it closely, Francis placed it back on the blanket with reverence. "I am a scientist. I would like to purchase this for my collection."

"I'm sorry, sir, this is not for sale, at any price."

"Would you allow me then, to take some measurements of it?"

"Yes, of course."

Francis took several precise measurement of the piece and reluctantly left the piece in the man's possession. He gave the man a business card and once again offered to pay the man handsomely for the artifact but to no avail.

As they walked back to the hotel, Francis and Mark discussed the Caduceus. "Was that as old as it looked?" Mark asked.

"Yes. It was amazing. I could swear I felt something odd when I held it."

"Odd?"

"Like, I don't know, electricity."

"You are obsessed."

"Yes, gladly so. I am convinced now that I am right, the Caduceus is not just a symbol but an ancient healing device. Moses made one, did you know?"

"Moses? Moses as in Charleston Heston Moses?"

"Yes, during the forty years in the desert, God told him to fashion a brass serpent around his staff and all those who touched it, looked at it, or drank from it, depending on your translation, were healed."

"I never heard that before."

"Exodus 4: 2-4. and Numbers, 21:8."

"You're religious?" Mark asked with incredulity.

"Not terribly, I just know about everything there is to know about the rod and the serpents. Cults sprang up that worshiped the Nehush'tan, the brass serpent Moses had made. The cult, however, was suppressed. Snake worship had too much in common with pagan beliefs. Also, the serpent was blamed for the expulsion of Adam and Eve from paradise. The serpent in paradise is always shown, by the way, wound around the tree of knowledge."

"So, you think it is a healing device of some sort?"

"Yes. Let me tell you why. First, the double helix is the staff of life in human existence. Then water is said to have healing properties when it achieves a spiral. Furthermore, the spiral universe in which we live may have some influence on the totality of life. When you add these together, the conclusion is inescapable, if you spiral water through a Caduceus, it may be healing. I hope to build my own Caduceus some day and now with these precise measurements, I'll get funding and build one when I get back."

"Oh, that reminds me," Mark said, "I got an e-mail from my ex-roommate. He wants to talk to you."

"What about?"

"He's gone off and become some kind of monk. Changed his name and moved to a small town in Arkansas. He's found some kind of healing spring or something. He said you would understand."

"Healing water?"

"Yes, he moved to Eureka Springs."

"The resort town?"

"Yeah, I don't know. He's gone a little crazy."

"Did he drop out of graduate school?" Francis asked.

"Dropped out of life. Calls himself Sanchi the Searcher."

"Hell, give him my e-mail. Maybe he's found something."

The two men walked into a plaza. Francis was rubbing his hand.

"What?" Mark asked.

"I don't know. It feels like a buzz, like when you touch a live wire."

"The Caduceus did that?"

"I'm not sure. The Caduceus has some strange properties. Some guy in Canada did research with a caduceus coil, he called it. He claimed it does some strange things."

"Strange how?"

"Levitation is one claim."

"Bullshit!"

"Caduceus coils have been reported to have resonating electric fields; no impedance or heating of wires when electricity is applied, levitation, strange personal effects, lost time, and lots of wild claims out there. Of course, mythology is replete with Caduceus stories."

"Mercury is holding one, isn't that right?"

"Yes, serpents wrapped around olive wood. The caduceus has many claims of alchemy and transformative powers, and some say it is an aphrodisiac. The rod as the male energy, the two serpents are female energies, linked together. One myth finds Tiresias discovering two snakes copulating and separated them with his staff. He was suddenly turned into a woman for seven years until he was able to repeat his actions and turned back into a man. Thus, the power of the two serpents and the staff became symbolic of transformation, from sickness to health, and death to life. The power was strong enough to transfer genders, male into female."

"You have been out in the hot sun too long."

"Hindus see the rod as the spine, and the serpents as chakra's that coil the spine. Occultists suggested the Hermetic nature of the Caduceus and attached it to their ceremonies."

"Hermetics?"

"Yes, that's seventh century lore, when Hermes became associated with alchemy. Alchemists were called sons of Hermes. There are occult relationships to the Caduceus in many cultures."

"That will make funding a lot easier." Mark said sarcastically.

"Did you say Eureka Springs?" Francis asked.

"Yes."

"Have him e-mail me. I'm always interested in water, particularly water that is healing."

"Your fascination with the Caduceus is really about healing, isn't it?" Mark asked.

"Yes. What if an ancient healing device is within our reach? What if all this mythology is not about symbolism, but is a link to a forgotten healing capacity of water?"

"Like I said, you've been in the hot sun too long." Mark patted him on the shoulder

Chapter 2

Eureka Springs Crescent Hotel
2002

Cassidy pushed the hair away from her face as she stood looking into the mirror above the sink in her hotel room. She was in Eureka Springs for a conference on aging. She was a hospice nurse and told her friends she chose to work with older people as a consequence of being raised by her grandparents. She liked older people and found herself more comfortable around people twice her age than with her contemporaries.

As she did her daily routine of twisting her hair into a wrapped knot, she began examining her face. She was nearly forty and for most of her life she had worn the countenance of a much younger woman. She studied the laugh lines around her eyes that lately had grown deeper. With the back side of her hand she pushed up on the area under her chin and watched in dismay as it sagged back into place.

Pulling a jar from her overnight bag she applied cosmetics and oils designed, or at least advertised, to restore the youthful elasticity of her aging skin. The mirror was old and beneath the glass the quick-silver had begun to flake away. Her reflection revealed a woman of character, strong cheek bones and light brownish-red hair. The red suggested a fiery personality could be contained within her. Beneath the surface of the hair she could see the telling signs of the white hairs coming back through the coloring.

She reached up to push the hairs beneath the surface.

"Just look at you," she said aloud. "You've turned into an old woman."

She bent over and splashed cold water on her face and grabbing a washcloth that had seen one too many washings, dabbed her face dry. She thought she saw a movement in the room as the light coming into the bathroom from the bedroom darkened then lightened as if someone had passed in front of the window.

The instinct of false modesty prompted Cassidy to grab a towel and clutch it to her chest – or perhaps the underlying need of protection urged the privacy of not exposing her breasts. She peered into the room.

"Hello!" she called out. There was no reply.

"Hello! Is there anyone there?" she called out again. The heavy brocade curtains moved as if blown by the wind, but the window was closed and locked. Cassidy cautiously stepped from the bathroom into the bedroom. Cold entered her body. Shudders rippled through her.

She stood still and took stock of her Crescent Hotel room. A fixture in Eureka Springs since the late 1800's, the hotel offered comfortable rooms decorated with a mixture of new furniture pieces designed to look as if they were from the turn of the century. She walked slowly to the window and looking out from the fourth floor, she could see the first light of morning touching the distant hillsides. The streets below her were colorful as local residents had maintained the Victorian appearances of the homes, bed and breakfast lodges and businesses.

The door to the bathroom banged shut and she jumped, dropping her towel. She walked toward the door and touching the handle, a feeling of dread came over her.

"This is silly," she said to herself. Pulling on the door she exposed the small room to the sunlight. The bath tub stood empty with the curtain pulled to the side. A small exhaust fan ran noisily. Surveying the floor with its zigzag design of small octagonal tiles, she reassured herself that the room is empty just as she had left it. She shook her head and returned to the mirror. Leaning close to inspect the wrinkles at her temples, she decided to put on some oil.

Retrieving a small glass bottle from her bag, she shook some of the oil onto her hand. "Oil of get laid," she laughed. Her brother called it that just to tease her. She looked up from her hands into the face of a stranger. Staring back at her was the apparition of a young woman. She was dressed in dark funerary clothes and her eyes were black. Her hand reached from inside the mirror toward Cassidy.

Cassidy shrieked, grabbed her towel, and running from the bathroom, pulled at the chain and lock that held her door closed. She tore her nails as she pushed the chain along the track and yanked it loose. Pulling the door open, she burst into the hallway.

"Are you all right?" a male voice behind her brought Cassidy abruptly into another reality. –

"Hell, no! I just had the fright of my life."

"I'm here in Eureka Springs to speak at the aging conference. I'm a water scientist and I'm fascinated with the medicinal springs here." Francis paused, "I'm sorry, I'm rambling, are you all right?" he asked Cassidy.

"Hell, no. I told you. There is something in my room." She emphatically gestured toward the room holding the towel in front of her. She noticed that Francis wasn't looking toward the room. Using both hands, she pulled the towel higher, "Don't look!"

"I'm not looking."

"The hell you weren't."

"I'm sorry, okay, I looked, I'm sorry. Do you want to come in my room and call the front desk?"

"I'm not going back in there." Cassidy pointed to her room.

Francis opened his door. He moved around the room straightening the top of the bed and moved his suitcase from the chair that was next to the phone stand. He handed her the phone. Cassidy was holding her towel with both hands so she made an exasperated face at him.

"You dial!" she grimaced at him.

Francis dialed the front desk. "Yes. Hello. I have a young lady here in my room –

No, that's fine – Listen she ran out into the hall and won't go back into her room. Yes,

I don't know – 419 I guess, no, I'm certain she was in 419. Well, I'm certain that will be no relief to her – Can you send someone up? When? Well, that won't do, I'm certain. I don't think after breakfast will work." Francis looked at Cassidy who was adamantly shaking her head no. "That won't do – can I what? Well, yes I suppose I could if that would be all right with Miss – I'm sorry, Miss, I don't know your name."

"Cassidy."

Francis spoke back to the phone. "Miss Cassidy. Yes, I'll see," Francis placed his hand over the mouth piece of the phone. "He wants to know if it would be all right with you if I went in the room with you. It seems they are a little short staffed for this kind of thing."

"What else did he say?"

"He said that this particular ghost is not harmful."

"Not harmful?"

"That's what he said."

"This particular ghost is not harmful?"

"Yes, that's what he said."

"And how many do they have?"

"He didn't say. What should I tell him?"

"Tell him I want another room."

Taking his hand off the phone he told the man at the other end that Cassidy wanted another room.

"They are full, he says."

"You tell him to find me another goddamn room right now!"

"She says….oh, you heard her. Well, all right, if it is okay with her."

"He says I can trade with you. Let's go back over there. You can put your stuff in my room until we switch. I don't mind really."

"You don't mind sharing your room with a ghost?"

"I meant I didn't mind sharing it with you, I mean, for just this morning. Actually, I have to get ready before too long. I'm speaking at the conference today."

"You go first." Cassidy pointed to her room.

"Perhaps I should introduce myself. I am Francis Allerton from the University of Missouri at Columbia." Francis held out his hand in an offer to shake, but Cassidy was holding tightly to her towel. She just nodded at him.

"Cassidy Martin, pleased to meet you. I work for Jasper County Hospice. I'm a nurse."

"Pleased to meet you. You're with Hospice? Don't you find the work, well, depressing?"

"Do you mind, Francis? I'm sitting in your room without a top, covered by a towel, I have to pee, and I just had a ghost come out of a mirror at me, could we skip the chit chat?"

"Well, sure, I'll go in first."

"Fine!" She lifted her hand and gestured toward the door across the hall. The towel slipped precariously close to the ends of her breasts. "You're looking again!"

"I'm not! I'm not! Really!"

Francis rose from his seat on the bed and walked across the hall way to room 419. The door had banged closed when Cassidy ran out, but now it hung open a few inches. Francis pushed the door open wide with one sweeping gesture. He took small steps as if he was creeping up on something across the room. He stood for a moment in front of the bathroom door and placed his hands on the door knob. He pushed the door open and went inside. Cassidy had leaned into the room keeping her feet in the hallway. Across the hall a woman came out of a room and walked toward her. She looked at Cassidy with disapproval as she passed her in the hall.

"Hell of an orgy last night. Too bad you missed it." Cassidy hissed at her. The woman hurried down the hall.

Francis returned to the doorway, "The friendly ghost is gone. You better get your stuff."

"Nothing in the mirror?"

"Just some handsome devil from Columbia."

"Oh, just get out of the way." Cassidy gathered her things, pushed them into her suitcase and giving a quick look around the room, shook her head and went across the hallway to Francis's room. "You didn't see anything?"

"You told me not to look."

"I don't mean that. I mean did you see anything in the bathroom mirror?"

"Sorry. Nothing."

"Don't be sorry. God! It was awful."

"I'm going to go down to breakfast. You can shower and get dressed."

"Don't leave me in this room by myself. Are you crazy?"

"Well, I thought you would be more comfortable, you know, with the looking thing and all that."

"Sit your ass down on that bed and don't move until I'm dressed. I'm going to go in the bathroom and get ready."

"Here, take this towel, to put over the mirror."

"Good idea. Seems college paid off for you."

"You're too kind."

"Don't mention it."

Francis sat on the bed with his back to the wall. He could hear Cassidy moving around in the bath room.

"Whistle!" she yelled out from behind the door.

"What?"

"Whistle. I have to pee and I can't go if you're sitting out there listening."

"For God's sake, what should I whistle?"

"God Bless America, who cares?"

Francis whistled. In a moment he heard the toilet flush. She swung the door open. She had dressed and was putting on eye makeup.

"What are you talking about today at the conference?"

"I'm giving a lecture on the spiritual essence of the dearly departed."

"Shut up!"

"Okay, I'm sorry that's not funny. I'm giving my talk on the chemistry of aging."

"Fascinating. That ought to keep them awake."

"Listen, this is fascinating to me. The chemical nature of aging is where all the research on aging is headed."

"You are right. I should be nicer to you. After all, you've seen me in a towel."

"I didn't look, well, not that much anyway. Not that they aren't worth looking at, I mean, had I actually seen them, they would be very nice I'm sure."

"You're sure?"

"If I had seen them, I'm sure they would have been spectacular."

"You are redeeming yourself, Mister Allerton, Francis, I mean. Okay, there, I'm ready for some breakfast. That's my life – see a ghost, run into the hallway without my top, meet a man, all before breakfast."

Chapter 3

The dining room was nicely laid out. The tablecloths were bleached white and the plates sparkled. Francis and Cassidy were seated near the doorway. She remained a little skittery from the morning.

"What kind of name is Cassidy anyway?" Francis asked as the coffee was brought to the table.

"Hollywood I guess."

"How so?"

"My dad loved Hopalong Cassidy, you know, the cowboy. So, when I came along he said that mom was in such labor pain that she couldn't walk into the hospital; she had to kind of hop along. I don't know. You just would have had to know my dad."

"I see. He has a sense of humor. I thought maybe it was for Butch, you know, Butch and Sundance."

"I get that a lot. Some of my friends call me Butch, but that's not such a flattering thing to call a lady."

"Depends on the lady, I guess. So, is that why you wear black?"

"No. I happen to look nice in black. It's not my only outfit."

"You look fine in it, I was just wondering if you tried to fit into the name. Some names have a lot of expectations wrapped up in them, like Junior for instance."

"I don't put a lot of stock into what other people think."

"Yeah, I heard you with that lady in the hallway this morning."

"I don't like judgmental people."

"Isn't that, well, kind of a judgment about them?"

"Shut up."

The breakfast came. Francis had bacon and eggs with wheat toast. Cassidy had an omelet the size of a trucker's breakfast. She ate about half of it and pushed the plate away.

"Want some?" she asked.

"I hardly know you." He replied.

Cassidy rolled her eyes. The waitress came back with coffee. She lingered.

"Yes?" Cassidy asked.

"You're the gal from Theodora's room?"

"Who's room?"

"Theodora. She was Doctor Baker's nurse and 419 was her room. That is the room that is most active."

"Active?"

"Yes. That's where most people see her. I saw her, too. They don't want us to talk about her much, the dark lady. But I saw her one morning before we opened up. I saw her at this very table. I thought someone had come in before we opened so I picked up the coffee pot and started over to her but before I got there she was gone. It scared me. I'm a good Christian so I don't want anything to do with the work of the devil."

"You think ghosts are the devil's work?"

"Of course they are. Everybody knows if you are righteous you go right on up to heaven when you die."

"Right on up, huh?"

"Yes, ma'm, right on up."

"So, there is some kind of elevator then?"

"No, ma'm, the angels come and get you."

"Not everyone, apparently."

"Well, I can tell I'm not talking to a Christian. Am I?"

"Well, not the kind that thinks everything we can't explain comes from the devil."

"Excuse me, ma'm, I won't bother you again. God bless you and come again."

The waitress turned and walked away. It seemed as if she was shaking her feet as if to kick off dust from them as she left the table. Cassidy rubbed her tongue between her lips and teeth as if she had just tasted something nasty.

"I hate that kind of crap."

"Crap?" Francis said.

"Oh, those Bible thumpers. We've got our share of them down in these sticks."

"Yeah. Hey, did you see that statue of Jesus as you came into town? It's mammoth!"

"Christ of the Ozarks, I think they call it. I wonder how Christ feels about becoming a tourist trap."

"I wouldn't think someone who had a near encounter with the hereafter would be so glib."

"Oh, I'm just sour on religion sometimes."

"People who don't believe in something will believe in anything."

"Who said that?"

"I don't know, but I think it's a pretty worthy sentiment."

A new waitress came to the table. "Will there be anything else?" she asked.

Francis responded first, "You know, I would like to have a bottle of the local water to take with me. The Ozark Valley Spring Water or whatever that name was. I don't want it from anywhere, just the water that comes from here."

"They don't bottle any of the local water anymore, sir. The springs are all running too low; perhaps it was in the fifties when they stopped bottling the local water." The waitress left the side of the table.

"You're a connoisseur of water?" Cassidy asked.

"Yes, of sorts. I have studied the water of this area. It is quite remarkable really. Water from here and from the Hot Springs area have quite a history to them."

"How so?"

"Well, would you believe that Desoto and his men came all the way to the White River area in search of the Fountain of Youth?"

"The actual Desoto?"

"Yes. His records indicated they came this far to the West and North before returning to the Hot Springs area. He had heard legends from Native Americans about the healing properties of the waters in Arkansas. What a trek that must have been, from Florida all the way to Arkansas."

"What did they find?"

"Well, that depends on which account of history you take as the truth. The water here is remarkable. It healed a lot of sick people. The Native Americans came here to take the waters, both to drink and to bathe in it. Reports were that both here and in Hot Springs warring tribes would put down their weapons and dispense with their hostilities when they were using the waters. Desoto referred to the area as the Valley of Peace."

"The world could use some of that today."

"Yes, exactly my feelings. It is part of my talk today, about water that is."

"You are going to try to get the leaders of the world to drink more water?"

"No. I'm afraid the state of water in America lends itself more to corruption than the opportunity for healing. I'm really speaking about the healing properties of water, in particular, the healing properties of spring waters with soluble minerals. There is this fabulous machine, from antiquity, called the Caduceus, that might also speed healing."

"I am aware that water has minerals. I went to nursing school, duh!"

"Yes, but only natural water has minerals."

"Isn't all water natural?"

"Well, yes and no."

"Which?"

"Most of it anymore, no."

"You are actually a serious scientist, aren't you?"

"Yes. I told you that earlier, when we met this morning."

"I wasn't in the mood to take in very much this morning, Francis. The ghost thing, remember?"

"Yes, I remember everything."

Francis let his eyes slip down toward Cassidy's chest. The gesture didn't go unnoticed.

"Keep your mind on your water!"

"Not all water is the same. You would be amazed to know what experiments are revealing about water lately."

"Water, water everywhere."

"Seriously, it may turn out to be the wonder drug and a key in the efforts to stop aging."

"So there is a Fountain of Youth?"

"Technically?"

"Yes, technically."

"Then I would have to say as a scientist, yes, there is."

"I'll take a pint. No, matter of fact, fill her up."

"If you attend my lecture today you'll learn what I am talking about. What time is it anyway?"

"It's nearly nine-thirty. When do you do your thing?"

"My thing, as you so nicely call it, is at eleven in the Conservatory on the first floor. Are you coming?"

"Not yet." Her double entendre didn't go unnoticed by Francis. "Is it like they said, the Fountain of Youth? When you drink it you turn back into a child?"

"No. It was never like that. It was more the case that if people drank of the healing water they stopped aging. There is some truth to the tales by the way."

"A drop of truth in an ocean of myth?" Cassidy made a curious association.

"More so like this. The Native Americans had a hard life and if you lived to thirty you were an old person. Modern medicine has only recently allowed people to reach their eighties and older. Native Americans that lived near healing springs warded off the diseases that afflicted the other tribes. When the other tribes would encounter them they seemed as if they were young people and biologically and physiologically, they were. They were spared the aging effects of various diseases and maladies that caused the others to age so quickly. Explorers were told the rumors of healing waters or perpetual youth and thus the legends of a Fountain of Youth in America were born."

"You are interesting. What a surprise."

"It's my best subject."

"Go on, I find this fascinating."

Francis was aware, perhaps the first time since they met, that Cassidy was actually sizing him up as he talked. He was a fairly handsome man, or at least that is what a few of his girl friends had told him. Having the audience of Cassidy spurred him on.

"Water is perhaps one of the most mythic substances on earth. It seems no accident that people are comprised of seventy percent water and that is exactly the estimate of the proportion of the earth's seas to its land mass, seventy percent. The notion that life on earth began in the sea is basically sound.

"Life depends heavily upon water. We think the best possible location for life in the universe would be on a planet or moon that contains water. Sitting across from me you are using water to live; your breathing, eating, drinking, digestion, elimination, all of them depend on water. The circulatory system is mostly water. The brain is the most important organ and it is primarily tissue and water. The capacity to store information and have a sense of self all depends on the ability of the brain to survive in that bubble of water in your head."

"So you're saying I'm a bubble head?"

"No. Listen to me. We regulate our moment to moment condition, our sweat and hydration all add up to a process that depends entirely on our water content. All that we do and become is water based. When you are in the womb, you are in a water protected environment. We begin life as a water breathing entity and it is only when we burst out of the womb we take our first breaths of air."

"So, you are kind of a nut case about water, aren't you?"

"Yes, I guess that's true. If you come to the lecture, you'll learn even more."

"Will there be an exam?"

"I could work something up, just for you. Are you going to come?"

"I can hardly keep from it. Do you want me to come, there I mean?"

"Yes. That would be great."

"Well, maybe if you beg."

"What?"

"Nothing, I'm just kidding around."

The second waitress brought a bottle of spring water to the table. "This is the water from the Hot Springs area."

"That will be fine." Francis smiled broadly at her.

Cassidy reached for the bill, "Let me pay for breakfast."

"No. That's not really necessary. I have an expense account. Let me put it on my room."

"Nope. You were nice enough to be my personal ghost buster, you let me use your room, and now I got the fifty cent lecture about water. I insist."

"You know what, I'll let you buy breakfast if you let me buy you lunch."

"Is this one of those conference things I have heard about, you know, the rendezvous?"

"Whatever you want to call it, just let me take you to lunch."

"Okay, Mister Allenton, you got yourself a date. I'll see you at the lecture. I expect to hear about this caduceus thing as well."

Francis smiled at her sweetly. He liked her and her odd ways. She was kind of smarty, quick-witted and not a bit dull. She had a fine face, pretty figure and a quick mind. He hoped lunch would lead to more.

Chapter 4

Eleven o'clock finally came after the morning had dragged through lectures and discussions about aging. Cassidy dreaded sitting through another lecture but was intrigued by Francis. She found the Conservatory on the opposite side of the hotel from the dining room through the reception area down a hallway. She took a seat near the back and watched as others chose seats in the bright sun that filled the room.

"May I have your attention, please." The moderator spoke loudly to the small but noisy crowd and waited a moment. "I am pleased to present Professor Francis Allenton. His topic today is 'The Chemical Basis for Aging'."

Polite applause rippled across the small crowd. Cassidy thought Francis looked strained. He retrieved a pile of notes from his inside jacket pocket and laid them on the steel podium. He pushed them around until he found a prearranged order. The crowd rustled with anticipation or was it boredom? He pulled a pair of horn-rimmed glasses from his outer jacket pocket and took a deep breath.

"I'm not accustomed to public speaking, but I wanted to talk at this conference today because I am convinced our knowledge of aging is moving in important directions concerning the chemical basis for the aging process.

"Let me review with you for a moment the present ideas about aging. First there is the theory of biological predisposition. Basically, these ideas suggest that every living organism has a hard-wired genetic code within the DNA. Once certain conditions are met, the code sends a message to the organism to age.

"Second is the notion that aging is a psychological phenomenon. I am a scientist and hold more to the arguments that can be observed in laboratory conditions. This theory places the responsibility within the aging person's mind. Age, in other words, is how you think and feel."

"Last, we come to my area of interest. Aging is a chemical interaction at the cellular level. I know this sounds a bit clinical and perhaps you have anticipated that I would trot out some kind of chemical formula for aging. In a way, you might be right.

"I was excited to learn that this conference would be taking place here in Eureka Springs. I have often wanted to visit this area, both for its scenic beauty but more importantly, for access to study the water.

"If you will sit back and relax for a moment, I want to help you walk a path with me about the fundamental importance of water and its relationship to aging. Let's start this walk thinking about water and the relationship water has to the life process of a cell. I don't want to be the first to break it to you, but you are a bunch of cells."

A few members of the audience chuckled. Francis continued, "Some of us have arranged them more nicely than others." Francis shot a quick glance at Cassidy. She smiled back.

"What a cell needs to do its work, basically to reproduce new cells that exactly mimic the original cell, is a source of energy. When you ate breakfast this morning, you, as a collection of cells, were replenishing the supply of materials you need to go on living. The cell needs proteins, vitamins, oxygen, and most of all, it needs minerals. The only way to get minerals into a productive and useful form is to suspend them in a water molecule. This is the only way a cell can consume minerals and make the energy required to sustain itself. No minerals, no cell growth. No cell growth is the clinical definition of death. A cell needs food to grow just like you do because you are, at a chemical and biological minimum, a bunch of cells.

"What do you need to have then, as a minimum, to live as a cell? Like the food pyramid suggested for a balanced daily diet, the cell requires the following things to thrive." Francis retrieved an overhead slide from a file on the table and turned on a projector.

"As you can see by this chart, a cell needs boron, chromium, copper, manganese, molybdenum, vanadium and zinc.

> Boron (boron citrate) ....3 mg
> Chromium ....400 mcg
> Copper...2 mg
> Manganese ....15 mg
> Molybdenum ....250 mcg
> Vanadium...7.5 mg
> Zinc...001 mg

"Not only does the cell require these elements to do its work, it requires them to be in small enough size, expressed as angstroms, to be used, and the only way that can happen is for them to be suspended in water molecules.

"I was telling a new friend this morning that our bodies are vessels comprised of about 70% water, and coincidentally, the world itself is a vessel comprised of about the same percentage or 70% water compared to land surface. I can see by the pained looks on some of your faces that I am losing you. Just bear with me one more moment, and I'll get to my point.

"Water needs to have certain bio-dynamic properties that allow it to pass freely through the cell membranes. When the cell is deprived of water, not just any water but water that has soluble minerals imbedded within it, it will age and eventually die.

"So, you can see, there really is a Fountain of Youth. It is water. How can that be, you will ask yourself, because all over the world people are drinking water and getting old? That's because they aren't drinking the right kind of water. Water that is generally available for direct human consumption has lost its vitality. It has been filtered, chlorinated, and changed from the basic water that greeted man when the world was young. Water that is primitive, pure and mineralized is actually still available in the world. You may not know, for instance, that the water captured as ice at the polar caps is water as old as the earth itself. Furthermore, well water, to be more precise, water from deep springs that was deposited hundreds of thousands of years ago, has the necessary suspended minerals to stop the aging process. The ancients knew this.

"Right here in Eureka Springs the Native Americans and the men who first drank and used the water to cure illnesses made a discovery that we have taken for granted. Water cures us. Not just any water, but deep spring water that has the necessary suspended minerals within it, not only cures us, but restores our cells to optimum health and prevents aging.

"Well, you may be asking yourself, why don't we just give everybody this miracle water and they will be well? In fact, history is replete with examples of healing waters. Lourdes in France is one example. Another is a spring in England that was said to flow from the hidden chamber that sprang forward when the Knights of Templar placed the Holy Grail within it. Those who drank from the red-tinted water reported miraculous cures for ailments and illnesses.

"The Bible is full of reports that relate to water. The Garden of Eden supposedly had a spring that flowed from its source and as long as Adam and Eve drank from it they would not have illness or age. When they were expelled from the Garden they began to show mortality, age and have illnesses.

"Christians in the audience will recall that Jesus referred to himself as the 'living water' and he was able to heal people and raise them from the dead. He walked on water; turned water into wine; and was transformed into God in the hands of John the Baptist when he was immersed into water. Some say the Great Flood cleansed the earth of evil. Across time, accounts about the search for the Holy Grail suggest that eternal life would bless the person who drank water from the cup. Stories about a Fountain of Youth have all painted the way, but we couldn't see it. How can the most universally available substance on earth be the very substance we need to fight disease and aging?

"So, I would submit, the answer for the disease of aging lies in water. Not just any water, but ancient water, with the proper soluble minerals in just the right combinations, created perhaps by accident as they percolate to the surface moving through strata and mineral-bearing rock with the right amount of heat and pressure. Water such as this is found right here in Eureka Springs and in Hot Springs. This is why Desoto and his band of men came all the way here from Florida, to find these springs and drink the water in 1541."

Francis reached for another overhead hoping to continue to hold their attention. "I have for you an analysis of the mineral content of the water bottled and sold for over a hundred years in Hot Springs.

Boron	3 mg
Chromium	400 mcg
Copper	2 mg
Manganese	27 mg
Iron	7mg
Molybdenum	250 mcg
Vanadium /lead	7.5 mg
Zinc	001 mg

"You will notice the strong resemblance to the chart I had up on the screen earlier. This water contains almost exactly the formula of cellular requirements for healthy growth and development. No wonder this water has been the water served to our Presidents since the 1950's when Eisenhower had a heart attack and told a news conference that he drank spring water on the recommendation of his physician. Actually, this spring water has been used by every President from Coolidge through Bush. I'm sure no one would be surprised to learn that a President from Arkansas would want to drink water from his native state. Our senators drink the same spring water. Perhaps they know something about the health benefits of this water, or perhaps it is just coincidence.

"Recently I have been working on a process that returns water to its natural, ancient state. I call it structured water and I am certain that it holds the greatest promise for combating the effects of aging. It has the life enhancing capacity that water used to have when the primal force of life ran through it. This bio-active water exists naturally in only a few places on earth and Eureka Springs used to be one of those. Unique geological conditions give rise to these springs and perhaps they have healing powers that other sources no longer have.

"For the most part, however, humans consume little beneficial water. Therefore, I thought I would offer you some consumer education about bottled water. Individuals around the globe consume some 89 billion liters of bottled water. Citizens of the U.S. consume about 13 billion liters of bottled water. When you consider that much of it is no more than bottled tap water, the profits are amazing.

"Multinational companies across the globe are collecting billions of dollars a year from bottled water. Companies are drilling high-capacity wells with plans to start bottled water plants whenever they wish. It is the only industry that is allowed to take a natural resource, owned by the public, and sell it back to them. Bottled water is the least regulated product of the food and beverage industry. The Natural Resources Defense Council found over a third of the brands that they tested contained arsenic and carcinogenic compounds.

"Global bottled water has exploded to a 35 billion dollar per year conglomerate. The United States market grew by over 13% in 2001. Americans paid $7.7 billion for bottled water last year. Less than a handful of companies control the world's bottled water supply. So much money and so little regulation naturally attract the attention of big business."

Francis gathered his notes and put them in his briefcase. He turned toward Cassidy as he finished his presentation. It seemed as if he was talking only to her.

"So, in conclusion, I wish each of you a long and productive life. Be cautious about what you're drinking and while you're in Arkansas, I encourage you to have a drink of spring water. Who knows, you might just wake up the next morning a younger and more vital person. I know I intend to."

Francis pulled a bottle of Arkansas spring water from his briefcase and taking off the top, he drank the entire bottle in front of the small crowd. When he finished it he looked directly at Cassidy.

"I'm feeling much younger now!" he said. His audience gave an enthusiastic applause.

The crowd thinned out with the exception of Cassidy and a man who stayed in his seat. He was well-dressed and seemed out of place.

"Well, how did I do?" Francis asked Cassidy.

"Great. I didn't know you were such a famous water scientist. I had no idea it had turned into such a large business."

"Modesty forbids me to brag. Does it turn you on?"

"Incurably."

"Then, yes, I am perhaps the most famous water scientist in the world."

The well-dressed man approached them. "Excuse me, Professor Allenton. I have a question."

"Certainly."

"I was concerned that the composition of the spring water from Hot Springs had lead and manganese in it."

"Yes, that's true. But they are in small amounts."

"Are you aware, sir, well perhaps you are, excuse me if I phrase this question in such a way as to insult your abilities."

"Please go on."

"Are you aware that these two minerals are known to produce aggressive behavior?"

"I am aware that some studies with incarcerated youth in England showed a correlation between certain minerals and aggression. Those studies, however, may be flawed."

The well-dressed man raised his voice slightly, "I beg to disagree. They used double-blind methods. Their results are unimpeachable."

"I'm certain you are more familiar with this research than I am." Francis responded to bring down the tension.

"Yes. I'm sorry. I'm just very interested in the subject of trace minerals in water and their behavioral consequences. I was wondering if I could offer you lunch, at my expense, of course."

"I have a previous engagement with this lovely lady. Perhaps another time."

"I'll be leaving for Washington shortly. Won't you reconsider?"

Cassidy sensed that this meeting was important for both men.

"Listen," she said. "I can grab my own lunch. You gentlemen go ahead and do your science thing."

"Are you certain?" Francis asked.

"Don't worry, we can have supper. I'll need the room key."

"Oh, yes, we are changing rooms, aren't we? Here you go. Six at the Crystal Dining Room then?"

"Six it is."

Cassidy left them talking and decided to go to the room. She went to the elevator and stood waiting as the mechanism came slowly to the ground floor. To her right a petite lady with a Crescent Hotel logo on her smock bent down on her knees and began dusting the floorboards. She looked up at Cassidy as the elevator clanked to a stop, "You're the one in Theodora's room?"

"Yes. Have I achieved fame around the hotel already?"

"The girls were talking at break. The waitress that got huffy with you, that's Marlena. She's got religion lately, well, actually it was just after she saw Theodora."

"That's what they call the ghost?"

"Some call her that. The room you are staying in was her room when Doctor Baker lived here. Some say she was such a good nurse she would never leave, feeling somehow that it was her duty both living and dead to watch over him."

"She was his nurse?"

"She cared for him as a nurse. That's the story." The woman returned to her cleaning duties around the base of the elevator. "She won't hurt you."

"Marlena?"

"No, silly. I mean Theodora. She's harmless."

"You've seen her?"

"No. I've seen things move, you know, from one place to another when no one was near them. I've seen books and things, candlesticks and chairs sometimes. They move from one place to the other."

"You don't find that strange?"

"Of course I do. The day it first happened I went home and put on a cross that I'd bought from one of the local shops, but after a while I decided that Theodora must not mean any harm. Not like the others."

"Others?"

"This town has its share of odd things. It sits above all those springs and caverns. It's an odd kind of place to live; all these Victorian homes and half of the people say they see things in them. But nowadays you can't be sure if they are telling the truth. People will come from all over to see a ghost and pay top dollar to stay in a place that has them. The ones you have to watch out for are the ones no one talks about. Those are the bad ones."

"So part of it is marketing and tourism, is it?"

"Yes, ma'm, it is. What a shame, too, people trying to cash in on those lost souls. It's not like the old days anymore when the springs ran strong and the waters cured people."

"Did they really cure people, I mean, from illnesses and disease?"

"Oh, yes. That's why we have so many people of faith living down here. They all thought the healings were signs of God or the second coming, and none of them wanted to miss it. Their families stayed in these parts after the original pilgrims came and died waiting for the end to happen."

"Is that why they have that giant Jesus across the hill?"

"It is partly the reason and partly not." She bent down to pick up a piece of paper on the floor.

"Partly not?" Cassidy asked.

"Well, you see, if there is a lot of evil in a place you need a lot of good to make it right for people that live there. We got a church right out the back door and you can see the Christ statue from out there, too. He's looking right at us, don't you know."

"Right at us?"

"Yes. There he is with his arms stretched out over the whole town. The religious folks decided it needed to be here and then there is that play they do. It seems that people around here need a lot of praying and religious things to make them feel safe at night."

"I see. You think they are here because they kind of balance out the evil things."

"Exactly!" The housekeeper returned to her duties.

"I heard that this town has a lot of old hippies and Buddhists, too."

"Oh, the flower people and the artsy-fartsy types are here, plenty of gays, too."

"Jesus stands watching over them, too, does he?"

"Oh, yes, they all need watching."

The elevator door had creaked open and waited empty. Cassidy noticed that the floor of the elevator was about four inches below the hotel floor. She decided to take the stairs instead.

Turning to her left she went up a massive staircase of aged, dark wood with light wood balusters on top of each post. Dark, Oriental carpet showed signs of wear and occasionally the floor dipped from the settling foundation. Cassidy walked down the fourth floor hallway past an observation deck, a lounge named for Doctor Baker and a meeting room under repair. She approached her room with caution and felt a little churning in her stomach as she put the key into the lock and turned it slowly to let herself in. The hair on her neck rose as she had her back turned to her old room. She closed the door behind her and lay down to take a nap.

Cassidy awoke close to five o'clock, fluffed her hair and repaired her eye make- up. She put on a black dress and added some sparkling earrings. Using the back stairway, she came out by the check-in desk. She turned toward the Crystal Dining room and passed a bar housed in a small room. A neatly lettered sign hung on the window, "Spirit Lounge."

"That's an understatement." She said to herself. Peeking in the doorway of the Crystal Dining room, she could see no one else was inside. She waited for twenty minutes before going to the front desk.

"Excuse me, sir." She addressed a man who was scurrying around behind the old counter.

"Yes, may I help you?"

"Are there any messages for me? I'm Cassidy Martin, room 426."

"I have a message for you, but you are in room 419, if I'm not mistaken? A gentleman is in 426."

"We changed rooms."

"News to me." He said with a grim smile.

"May I have the message anyway?"

"Certainly, you seem to be who you are."

Cassidy shook her head, but decided to allow the man his discomfort with the room change. She hadn't called anyone herself, but thought the matter had been handled by the call Francis had made earlier in the morning. The note she now held in her hand was folded neatly. She opened it and read, "Call your friend, Dr. Marianna Dean as soon as possible."

Cassidy worked with Dr. Marianna Dean. They had developed a special friendship. Hospice work was difficult and Dr. Dean was not afraid to prescribe pain killing medications at doses high enough to bring an end to the pain of those who were facing death. Deep friendships developed between hospice workers and they pulled no punches with each other. Cassidy, as well as many others, found that one of the ways to deal with the constant presence of death in Hospice work was to develop a dark sense of humor. Recently, although she had a regular general practitioner, when Cassidy needed a biopsy on her breast, it was Marianna Dean that she went to. She knew and trusted her. Cassidy pulled out her cell phone, slowly walked over to an empty corner of the lounge by the windows, and selected Marianna's direct number.

"Hello." Dean's familiar voice rang out.

"Hello, yourself."

"Cassidy, how's it going? How are you feeling?"

"I'm fine. I met a man, of all things."

"Stay off your back, girlfriend!"

"Shut up!"

"How far did you go?"

"He saw my tits."

A tense silence took over the conversation.

"Well, are you going to tell me or not?" Cassidy asked.

"It's not good."

"Like I thought?"

"Yes. I'm sorry, Hon."

"How long have I got?"

"Who can say? Listen, get yourself back up here. There are some things I think we can do. I have a friend at Sloan-Kettering I want you to see."

"That bad, huh?"

"You can lick this, Cass."

"Yeah, me and what army?"

"Cassidy, I'm serious. You need to get back here as soon as you can."

"I hear you, but will a day or so really matter anyway? No, I'll finish what I started here. What a pain in the ass! I don't see why now and why me. Hell, I never even smoked or breathed others' smoke."

"I know. It's not fair. Listen. Call me when you start home. I mean it."

"I'll call you. By the way, I saw a ghost today."

"Stop it!"

"See, even when I'm serious you think I'm jerking you around."

"Whatever."

"You didn't say, by the way, how long?"

"I know."

"You can't tell me."

"I won't tell you. We have a lot of work to do. I hate this, Hon."

"Not more than I do."

"Maybe. Well, call me."

"Okay, I will. I'll see you soon."

"Bye."

Cassidy found an over-stuffed seat and flopped down on it. When her shaking knees calmed down, she slipped through the back door. To the East she could see the Christ statue catching the light of the late afternoon sun.

"I could use a little help over here!" she shouted toward the statue then looked around to make sure she was alone. The fresh air seemed to help.

Taking a deep breath, she slowly descended the back steps and walked toward the church nestled below the hotel. Crossing the narrow road, she approached a stone gazebo structure that held a statue of Mary. The sun was dropping behind the hills and a cool breeze came up.

Looking down, Cassidy saw Francis hurrying up steps behind the church. He hesitated long enough to light a cigarette.

"Those will kill you!" she yelled at him.

"Cassidy! Stay there, I'll come up. I'm sorry. I know I'm late. Stay there."

"No, you stay there. I could use a little company and I've lost my appetite."

She walked down to him and brashly took the cigarette out of his mouth. She flipped it down the hillside.

"They can kill you, take it from me."

"You look as if you have seen a...."

"Ghost?"

"Well, frankly, yes. Are you all right? Did you see the woman in the mirror again?"

"You mean Theodora? She has a name you know?"

"They have so many that they name them?"

"Where have you been? Making holy water for the Catholics?"

"That's sick."

"I'm in no mood to be proper."

"The evening isn't over then?"

"Well, we have already shared so much; a ghost, me streaking in the hall, breakfast, a lecture, being stood-up for supper."

"I couldn't help it. This guy had quite a story and maybe a job offer for me."

"The guy from Washington?"

"Yeah. There is a research project waiting approval."

The night air turned chilly. Cassidy shivered, perhaps because of the air or the ghost or because she was standing next to a man that found her interesting, or perhaps because the hand that reached for her today from the mirror was death itself.

Chapter 5

"I'm going to go upstairs now, to my room."

"That's our room, isn't it?" Francis said.

"Well, for tonight let's call it my room."

"Can I check on you? I have an appointment around nine."

"Sure, come up and knock on the door."

Cassidy went to her room and pushed on the door. Her bags were piled in the corner and Francis's belongings remained where they were before breakfast. A voice from behind startled her.

"Professor Allenton?"

She turned to see a man dressed as a Buddhist Monk standing in the doorway.

"No. I mean this is his room. I am a friend of his."

"As you say. I had an appointment with him for nine tonight."

"Nine? You are a little early."

"Yes. Truly, I was so looking forward to talking with him. He is a genius when it comes to certain things. Perhaps you can help me find him. Friends know a way when others falter."

"You were going to talk about water, doubtlessly?"

"Yes, this is truly so. Water and the mysteries of the world, and I was so looking forward to it. Well, all things happen as they should. I'll be going now, a blessing on you."

"Wait a minute!"

"Excuse me?"

"I was wondering, when I see him, how he might find you, so he can keep his appointment with you?

"I run a small book and incense store in the main shopping area. He will find the way. A man on a journey finds the path that he must travel. Either sooner or at a later time we will have our time together." The Monk turned to go. He stopped and pivoted on the balls of his feet. "I have a feeling about you, Miss."

"A feeling?"

"It seems as if the hand of God is all around you."

"Great," she thought to herself, "two men interested in me and they both are nuts."

Cassidy picked up the phone and called the front desk.

"Front desk." A voice offered.

"Is Francis Allenton down there by the desk?"

"One moment please – No, ma'm. Would you like his room?"

"No, I'm in his freakin' room."

She hung up and looked at her watch. It was nearly nine. "I'll go down with you. I know what he looks like."

"As you wish."

Cassidy and the monk went down the steps. The same housekeeper Cassidy had visited with earlier was standing in the doorway as if she were waiting for a ride.

Cassidy spoke, "Hello, again. I was wondering, did you see the man I was with earlier today?"

"Yes. He just left the hotel in the company of another man about quarter to nine."

"Are you sure?"

"Honey, that's what I saw. He was with a man dressed just like this man."

Cassidy and the Monk looked at each other.

"That can't be," he said. "I am the only Monk in this town."

"Which way did they go?"

"They went toward town on the low road. They were walking."

Cassidy and the Monk started out after them.

Chapter 6

Francis and his new contact had started down the hill at a fast pace. The Monk initiated the conversation, "Thank you for meeting with me, Professor Allenton. I am Sanshi Ravanashi."

"It's my pleasure. I was intrigued by your e-mail."

"How so?"

"Your discovery of the hidden spring and the possibility that it might remain a healing spring caused me quite a stir. How did you find it?"

"I was looking at some records in the town hall, when the town was first laid out they took extra careful efforts to insure the protection of the springs."

"That was a wise precaution."

"It was prudent of them. The founders of this town knew the value was in the water as opposed to the land. I found an old reference to a deep water spring that lay just outside of town, too far perhaps to capitalize on it with a bath house or spa."

"It's out of town then?"

"Just a mile or so."

"Why did you contact me?"

"Your work on primitive water was fascinating."

"I'm curious, why a Buddhist Monk would care about water in the first place?"

"We believe, unlike the western mind, that water is alive. Not in the scientific sense that it contains elements and molecules that are alive, rather, in the very real sense of a living sentient being."

"Water science has similar beliefs in certain circles but mostly the study of water falls into a chemical rather than cosmological study."

"Your work to reinvigorate water to a more primitive and healing state may offer much promise to mankind."

"There is very little primitive water left in the world. You have to come to places like this. Overpopulation and excessive use have dropped the water table so far down that the healing springs remain mostly under the water table and the little bit that reaches the surface is contaminated by ground source pollution." Francis paused, then added,

"How deep is the spring?"

"I have not taken any measurements as I do not have the kind of equipment or resources to do so. I found the spring and didn't want it to be gobbled up by the business-minded. A healing source like this is always at risk of being exploited. I have obtained a sample for you as requested."

"How old is the sample?"

"It is less than seventy-two hours, as you requested."

"I'll be able to do a preliminary analysis on it back in my room."

"I put my telephone number on the label of the vial."

"You kept the vial as I instructed. I don't want a contaminated sample."

"I did exactly as you instructed. How long will your analysis take?"

"I can do a preliminary review in a few hours, but I need my lab to do the complete analysis. When can I see it?"

"I will reveal the source of the spring to you when you have given me the full analysis."

"That wasn't our arrangement. I thought you would take me to the source during my visit here."

"None the less, this is how things must go now."

"Have I done something to offend you in some way?"

"No. I need to protect the source. It is a difficult process. We are negotiating to purchase the land and I need to be certain that the water has curative powers. If anything gets out or if anyone suspects the true nature of the spring, the purchase will fall apart. We need absolute secrecy in this matter."

The path the Monk had taken led back uphill to the front of the hotel. "I'll leave you here then, Professor Allenton. It was a pleasure to meet you in person."

"Thank you. I will contact you with my complete analysis."

"You will call me at the number I gave you."

"I can e-mail you the results."

"I don't trust the e-mails anymore. People can find their way into your e-mail and steal your secrets. You must delete that e-mail address and don't respond to anyone who may communicate to you from that location."

"You suspect someone is aware of the spring?"

"I suspect it is possible for things to get out. I'll hear from you then soon."

The monk turned and walked into the night. Francis went into the hotel and up the steps to his room. He held the key for 419 in his hand. He didn't like the prospect of sleeping in that room. He walked across the hall and tapped on the door to his old room. No one answered. His luggage was in the room so it was irritating to him that he couldn't get to his bag. He decided to go to the main desk to see if he could get a key for his former room.

"Hello." He called out to the empty front desk. A sleepy-looking older man emerged.

"Yes sir?"

"I would like a key to my room, 426."

"Your name, sir?"

"Allenton, Francis Allenton."

The man looked in the registry. Peering over his glasses he looked back at the book.

"Says Cassidy Martin is in 426 here in the book, sir."

"Yes, I know. I traded my room with the young lady earlier today. My bags and things are still in the room."

"I wouldn't have any authority to let you back in that room now, sir. She's probably in there asleep."

"No. I knocked on the door and she didn't answer."

"She might be asleep, sir."

"Could you ring the room then?"

"It is against our policy, sir, to call rooms after midnight. Perhaps you can just wait until the morning."

"I can't wait. I have some items in my room that I need now."

"I'm sorry, sir. I can't let you in the lady's room at this hour."

"Fine. That's just fine. Thank you for all the help."

The clerk gave him a strained smile and went back behind the partition. Francis looked at the key to 419 in his hand. He decided to step outside on the back veranda and take a smoke and calm himself down.

Chapter 7

"Where does this road lead?" Cassidy asked the monk.

"It goes downtown but there are at least a dozen side roads that come off of it."

"Do you see them?"

"I see nothing. A man in the dark, however, can see more than his eyes reveal."

"Is it a prerequisite for monks to talk that way?"

"What way?"

"Never mind. Why does a monk live in Eureka Springs?"

"Why indeed does a monk live anyplace?"

"Mystics always have a way of answering a question with a question."

"I see, you are asking me why I live here in this place?"

"See, another question."

"I seek enlightenment and a path to knowledge."

"And a meeting with Professor Allenton will bring this to you?"

"He and I enjoy a bond. We have been talking by e-mail. He is a colleague of my former college roommate."

"Monks use e-mail?"

"We both see the healing potential of water."

"I see. You both are obsessed with water."

"Water is the answer."

"To what question?"

"Water is given by God to bring healing and comfort. Water has been corrupted by man's influence, but it may be possible to return it to a harmonious state with the Creator and thus, restore it to its natural state bringing healing and comfort to the afflicted."

"You are going to sell this wonder cure?"

"I have no interest in money for the water. I am interested in giving it to the world if the water I have found is capable of such regeneration."

"You have found a healing spring?"

"I have found a spring, thanks be to God. I work part-time to help support our temple. I was working to repair some mortar and stone that had crumbled in the church that lies below the hotel. This town has a lot of subsidence due to the springs undermining the soils. The church has a Holy Water caldron that has been there as long as the church. You perhaps noticed the dome-like structure on the side of the church?

"I didn't really pay very much attention to it."

"I was repairing the stones around the caldron as they had fallen in when some of the ground gave way below them. As I pushed the stone altar aside, the stones fell into a deep hole. I found a set of ancient stairs carved into the walls beneath the area where I was working. I could see they went to a deep cavern. Something inside of me told me to go there."

"Well, what a surprise. A church is hiding something."

"I have no judgments of them. Perhaps the present priests are unaware of this hidden area. I descended the steps until they stopped at an ancient altar. Some symbols were inscribed on a stone: a spiral with balls, some serpents entwined around a rod, and a fish. I had a bottle of water with me so I dumped it out and filled the bottle with the water from the well. I was very excited. It is deep enough to perhaps be the same water that was used to heal people in this area before the water disappeared back beneath the ground. I replaced the covering and made a repair that only cosmetically closed the opening. I can get back down there again since they think I still have repairs to do."

"This is the water you wanted to talk to Francis about? Does it heal the sick?"

"This I do not know. I need Professor Allenton to tell me if it has the potential to be regenerated as primal healing water. The springs in this area healed many people when they were first discovered, but greed and overuse have taken their powers away. When people attempt to profit from God's gifts, they are taken away."

"God has franchise rights?"

"You have bitterness toward God."

"He has bitterness toward me it seems."

"You have darkness around your spirit."

"It's night time."

"It serves you poorly to bite the hand of kindness."

Cassidy and the Monk turned a corner. The older Victorian homes caught the moonlight in the fancy bric-a-brac work on their porches. They walked in silence passing several homes.

"I need to sit down for a moment." Cassidy broke the silence.

"You are not well?"

"I didn't have supper and I had a bit of a misadventure this morning."

"A sign, perhaps."

"A sign?"

"God sends us signs to help us find the pathway to Him."

"I can wait."

"You do not seek enlightenment?"

"I am open to learn, but I can wait to see God."

"You fear death."

"Like a Jehovah Witness at the door."

"You are angry with God."

"He's a bully."

"We are what we see in the Divine."

"I don't think so. Listen, I don't want to stand here and play twenty cosmic questions. Okay?"

"Shall we walk on then?"

"Yes. Let's head back to the hotel. Maybe Francis came back that way."

They walked again in silence. Their feet made hollow sounds as they stepped on stone sidewalks. The stones were uneven, some pushed up from below and some sunken. Cassidy stubbed her feet more than once. She decided to ask the question that kept rolling around in her head, "What's the Buddhist take on ghosts?"

"We accept the place of all things. Some things find their resting place and some continue to search. A ghost is a soul that is searching for enlightenment."

"You don't see them as either good or evil?"

"We do not see things in the duality of good and evil, they are what they are."

"So there is no evil?"

"Evil is one thing to one person and something else to another."

"And what's your view on death?"

"Death is the place to which all mankind is moving. Life is transitory and fleeting. This is the second time we have talked of death tonight. Is there something facing you?"

"Not if I run quick enough."

They arrived back at the front of the Crescent Hotel. The large copper crescent shone in the moonlight.

"I don't know what to tell you…Mister, ah, did you tell me your name?"

"I didn't. It is Sanshi."

"Well, Sanshi, I don't know what to tell you about Francis. Do you want to come up to the room and see if he is back?"

"I will leave you now. I will talk with him tomorrow. May your heart find rest tonight."

"Thank you." Cassidy said turning and going up the large steps to the double doors. She opened the door and then turned to wave at Sanshi, but he was standing by a car with his back to her. The back window was down and he was talking to someone. He placed his hand on the door handle and then slowly opened the door and climbed in the back seat next to another gentleman. Cassidy came back out the door, but the car squealed off into the dark.

The interior of the car was dark. A voice spoke from behind the darkness.

"Are you Sanshi?"

"If it pleases you."

"You can't put that mystical crap back in the bag where you got it. Are you Sanshi?"

"It must be so or why else would we be talking."

"You have been sending messages to a Doctor Allenton."

"As you say."

"What you are doing is a threat to the safety of the United States."

"I am Peace, surrounded by Peace. I dwell in the safety of Peace for it is above me, below me and within me. When such Peace is mine, all is well."

"Peace is not the business of people like you. Peace is the work of larger people who want larger things."

"When there is Peace, it is between all things and all people. Peace does not belong to any man but to all men."

"Where is the spring you spoke of to Professor Allenton?"

"The Earth holds many treasures."

"We have our ways to get information out of you. You will be better off if you tell me what I want to know."

Sanshi assumed a lotus position on the car seat. "I pray that you shall learn Karuna, pity for all who suffer. No man or woman suffers alone. Where are you taking me?"

"We have a place for people who threaten the safety of the world."

"Then I must be going in your company."

The car drove off into the darkness moving toward the far end of an airport south of Branson.

Cassidy had watched the car drive away with Sanshi inside. Tiredness overwhelmed her. She had gone without supper and missed a pain pill. She began to feel the pain well up inside her again. She hated how the pill made her feel light in the head, but it pushed the pain aside. She waited for the elevator. This time the elevator stopped even with the floor.

She was glad that she hadn't taken the stairs. For a moment she stood in front of her old room debating whether to knock. She hated the idea of going back into that room. She knocked, but when Francis did not answer the door, she was partially relieved and partially concerned. She turned to open the door to her new room, thanks to his generosity, and heard footsteps coming up the back stairwell.

"Francis, thank God." she said no longer holding her breath.

"That's what a man likes to hear when a beautiful lady sees him."

"Where did you go and with whom?"

"Jealous already? This will never work out."

"No. I'm not jealous. I just took a turn around town with a Buddhist Monk named Sanshi. We were looking for you."

"That's not possible. I just had a meeting with him."

"So you think."

"Listen, this isn't funny."

"I'm not kidding. I was downstairs and heard him ask for you. The housekeeper told us you had just left with a man dressed like a monk."

"He is a monk. That's why he dresses like one. What did your guy look like?" Francis pressed the point.

"Eisenhower! Like a monk, what do you think he looked like?"

"Well, I don't understand. Where is your guy now?"

"He took off in a car with some men, although it didn't look to me like he wanted to go with them."

"So he's not here anymore?"

"No. I'm not making this up."

"What did he tell you?"

"You and he and the secret water spring, you know, just a few things you forgot to mention to me, since I'm your best new friend and you've seen my tits."

"What did you tell him?"

"Nothing! What do I know to tell him?"

They stood for a moment in silence. Francis sighed. "I need my stuff from your room, well actually, my room."

"Fine. Come in and get it. I'm dead."

"No, that would be your friend from this morning."

"Francis, you are not funny either."

"Well, come on then, Cassidy, where did you go really and with whom?"

"I told you, Francis. Why would I lie to you?"

"Why indeed?"

"Don't answer a question with a question."

"Don't tell me how to talk."

"Okay. Look! I'm tired and not feeling all that well. Come in and get your stuff and go spend the night with Theodora or whoever she is and in the middle of the night if she puts a sheet up your ass, don't call me."

"Fine! Just let me get my bag." Francis came into the room and gathered his things. He went out the door and pushed his key into the lock.

"No kiss goodnight?" Cassidy called behind him.

Francis hunched his shoulders as if he was about to say something, but he loosened his posture and turned to face her. The light was on her hair from the hallway and her face looked very haggard.

"Are you all right? Can I get you something?" His voice was suddenly more tender.

"A good night's sleep will do it for me. Do you have anything to eat?"

"I have some crackers. You know, the ones with peanut butter on them?"

"Hand them over." She put out her hand.

Francis sat his suitcase on the floor and unzipped the side. A water analysis kit fell out on the floor. He quickly gathered it back together and fishing in a side pocket produced the bright orange crackers in a cellophane wrapper.

"Health food. Remember, you are what you eat." He said as he handed them to her.

"Got any of that life-giving water left on you?" Cassidy asked. She thought his face flushed, embarrassed as if he had just been caught doing something improper.

"No. Sorry. Fresh out tonight. Have a good night and try to avoid the paranormal."

"There is nothing normal about me, I assure you, Professor Allenton, nothing normal at all." Then she surprised herself by repeating the monk's departing words.

"May your heart find peace."

In her room Cassidy lay on the bed and let herself fall asleep fully clothed. She didn't want to risk jumping up at night and running into the hallway undressed if Theodora came calling.

Francis set up his water analysis kit for a preliminary examination. He went into the bathroom and seeing himself walk by the mirror gave himself a scare.

"Jeeez!" he said out loud, "I look beat." Then looking out the window he could see the statue of Christ visible throughout the night with flood lights. "Sorry!" he called out to it.

His alarm awoke him at 3 a.m. He didn't immediately remember why, but he turned on the light and looked across the room at the field test of the water sample. Looking closer he was puzzled. Nothing seemed remarkable at all. The sample analyzed as ordinary as most bottled spring waters sold all around town. Troubled and disappointed, Francis decided he needed to call the number the Monk had given him. The phone rang once and was immediately answered.

"Sanshi here."

"Sanshi, this is Francis. I'm concerned about the results."

"Yes. Go on."

"It's flat. It is as ordinary as most water around town."

"I am deeply sorry to have troubled you sir. I shall not bother you again."

"Did you sterilize the collection jar, like I told you?"

"I did as you said."

"Did you collect the sample from the deep water in the pool?"

"I did as you said in the e-mail."

"Well, I'm sorry to tell you this, but there is nothing extraordinary about the spring."

"As I said, I shall not trouble you again."

"Perhaps if I visited the site."

"That is not possible. Good night, sir. It's quite late."

"Sanshi, let me ask you a question. Are there any more monks in town?"

"There are none but me, a humble servant of God."

"Perhaps I could take my own sample – " The telephone line was empty on the other end.

"Something's not right about this." Francis said aloud as he climbed back into bed.

Chapter 8

Francis tapped on the door across the hall. It was 8 o'clock and he thought he could hear stirring inside. The door swung open wide to reveal Cassidy in a robe with a towel around her head. He greeted her first, "Good Morning. Let's get some real food in you. You even look good in the morning."

"You sound surprised. Did you have a visitor last night? What is sex like with a dead woman?"

"About like my last girlfriend, I should guess."

"That's mean."

"The truth can be cruel."

"Did you figure out who you went strolling around with last night?"

"I went with the monk, but I'm feeling a little odd about the whole thing. I did a preliminary analysis of the water sample he gave me and there is nothing to it."

"Tell me about it at breakfast. I could eat the ass end out of an elephant."

"Ah, the delicate feminine approach to life. It is most refreshing."

"Give me a few moments to get ready." Cassidy grabbed some clothes and went into the bathroom.

"Anybody else in there with you this morning?" Francis teased her from outside the door when he heard the hair dryer stop.

"Did you see anything in Theodora's room?"

"Nothing to compare to what I saw yesterday morning."

"Shut up! That was, well, to say the least, embarrassing."

"Hey, you should be proud of those. I thought nurses were, well, more open-minded about nudity."

"Great! I thought you said you didn't look."

"I didn't say I didn't see anything. I just said I didn't look."

"Could we change the subject?" Cassidy felt uncomfortable talking about her breasts. She wasn't a prude but since they were the location of her recently diagnosed cancer, she wasn't sure how she felt about them. She certainly didn't want to think about a future breast removal this morning. "Is that all you see in a woman? Her boobs?"

"Well, honestly, no. But so far that's all I have seen of you. Come on, I'm just teasing."

"I was just wondering. I mean, how do you think it goes between a man and woman when one of them gets sick or if the woman has to have surgery?"

"I think it depends on the couple. My mom had a breast removed and a reconstruction. Dad told me it was difficult for a while. She didn't want to be touched or seen, but they worked through it. I don't know but it seems to me they loved each other a long time and the love was stronger than the losses."

"That's sweet." Cassidy said as she emerged from the bathroom.

They walked down the steps together and into the diningroom. A Sunday buffet was set so they decided to get in line. The room was only half-full so they could take a seat by the windows with a view. The waitress that huffed off the day before came up to them again.

"Morning, Miss. Will you be having coffee?"

"Yes. I would also like a bottle of that spring water. Mister Allenton here has convinced me that I would be better off with spring water to drink. Who knows, it might cure me."

"You need curing?" Francis asked.

"Don't we all?" Cassidy replied.

They both ate a very large breakfast without much conversation. When the bottle of water was set on the table, Cassidy opened it and poured some into a small juice glass.

Francis reached over, picked up the bottle, and reading the label said, "People don't really know what they are drinking when they buy bottled water. Much of it isn't spring water, you know."

"They're everywhere, aren't they?" Cassidy replied.

"I can't go anyplace that people aren't toting water bottles around. Bottled water is the fastest growing segment of the food and beverage industry."

"The regular water isn't safe anymore."

"Don't fall for that. They are as good at pushing water as they are at pushing cola. Do you realize that people are paying one thousand percent more for water than the cost of tap water and for the most part they are getting the same thing?"

"Let me ask you, because I don't really understand, what's the difference between mineral water, bottled water, spring water and the like?"

"You're not going to fall asleep on me are you if I explain it?"

"Just give me the dime tour."

"Okay. Mineral water is underground water protected against pollutants and characterized by a constant level of minerals and trace elements. It cannot be treated or minerals added.

Spring water is derived from an underground formation from which water flows naturally to the surface. Spring water must be collected only at the spring or through a bore hole tapping the underground formation that feeds the spring. Water from different springs can be sold under the same brand name."

"What is well water? That's what I have at home. I live in a small community that has a shared well. I thought well water was the same as spring water."

"Well water is from a hole drilled into the ground that taps an aquifer. An aquifer could be any porous set of rocks that traps runoff water from the surface, such as rain, or other types of runoff. It is the most susceptible to pollution depending on what the water must run through in order to locate itself in the aquifer."

"I know what city water is. Drawn from an impoundment, like a lake, or recycled water from use upstream."

"Yes, that's right and it is vulnerable to a number of sources of pollution. It is perhaps the most treated of all water, and it should be. There is one other source and that is desalted water, such as that used by countries in the Far East. Libya, Israel, Palestine, and Saudi Arabia all use desalting."

"I grew up on a farm that had a cistern. We used to catch rain water. It made your hair feel so soft."

"Rain water has become toxic as the atmosphere has become polluted. Some water scientists feel that most of the modern human illnesses can be traced to pollution in the water system. Then there's the fluoride controversy. Some say fluoride's side effects are dangerous. Others feel it is an extremely important additive to drinking water."

"I'm going to owe you more than a dime for this explanation. Let me ask you, seriously now, do they think disease, say cancer for instance, is from the water?"

"Depends who you talk to."

"What do you say?"

"I think the increase in bottled water consumption by the world is in response to a basic instinctual realization that our water supply does not do the work of sustaining and replenishing our bodies and on some level people know this and are seeking a solution. Add the high level of marketing and the blitz of available water supplies in stores and vending machines and you have an amazing phenomenon. It's a billion dollar industry now. I never saw people drinking bottle water just a few years ago. Now it is everywhere. Consumption goes up by 12 percent a year and over the last 30 years it is up thousands of percent, particularly in North America. Nearly 60 percent of Americans drink an average of 15 liters of bottled water per person per year, but that's even less than Europe's 88 liters per person.

"On the world level it has reached ninety billion liters a year, and well over 22 billion dollars are spent by consumers on water. Sixty percent of that is just purified tap water. Three-quarters of the world's bottled water is produced by a handful of companies."

"Now I owe you a dollar." Cassidy said. "Listen, I have another question."

"You have been listening!"

"Shut up! Really, you said that none of it is regulated, you know, controlled by any one at an official level. Is that right?"

"Essentially that is correct."

"Then how do you know which water to buy?"

"Consumers are making choices based on marketing and scare tactics. Many believe that tap water is unsafe."

"Isn't that true?"

"Not in the least. There is very little evidence to prove tap water in this country is less healthy than bottled water. Actually, no standard exists for the mineral content of water. Although we think certain minerals promote better health, there are no standards to set to indicate which minerals produce what health benefits. Minimum criteria levels for mineralized water are being reviewed by Codex, an international arm of the World Health Organization, but they have not made a determination yet."

"So, should we all just save our money and drink out of the tap?"

"That all depends on who you are talking to."

"I'm talking to you."

"I do have some concerns about municipal water supplies. You're on a well, you said?"

"Yes."

"I would have to come to your house, assess the draw area, look at the environmental hazards, do a study of drainage, look at the septic discharge adequacy and then I could tell you."

"Nothing like shooting from the hip."

"Then I would draw three samples from three sources on the feed lines and two at various locations in your house. Depending on the results I would be able to devise a purification system for you."

"Hey, Culligan Man!"

"You asked the question!"

"I know. I'm just kidding around. It is serious science, isn't it?"

"Get into something that everybody needs. That's what my dad used to tell me."

"Mine told me to get into poverty or health care. He used to say that's where all the money is. I get the water thing though, really. As a nurse I see a lot of things that good hydration could help. Two liters a day a person needs, right?"

"Yes. Who's the bright one now?"

"I thought the Government did regulate water consumption, or at least water use."

"Local and state governments, as well as the federal government, have increasingly become active in regulations about water use. As they prevent people from certain use patterns from reservoirs, for instance, people turn to bottled water. We consumed 43 billion 16 ounce bottles last year."

Francis' cell phone interrupted. "Excuse me, will you? I am expecting a call."

He rose and went to the corner of the room. He didn't recognize the caller's number on his screen.

"Hello."

"Is this Professor Allenton?"

"You got me."

"Professor Francis Allenton?"

"Right again."

"This is Alford Purlough of the Codex Alimentarius Commission. I spoke to you yesterday following your presentation."

"I had no idea you were with the CAC when we spoke. It's an honor to have you come to my presentation."

"No. Not at all. The honor was mine. I was wondering if you would be willing to speak with me again in person about the research project. We are definitely seeking a principal investigator and I would like to discuss further your interest in this. If I understood what you said yesterday, your university contract is not tenured and may not be renewed. Is that right?"

"Yes, that's right."

"The project I spoke with you about yesterday has now expanded. I discussed your qualifications with my colleagues following our meeting yesterday. We are all very excited about moving forward. In fact, I stayed over in Eureka Springs just to discuss this further with you. Are you free just now?"

"I'm visiting with a lovely young lady at the moment. I can get free in say, fifteen minutes."

"Fine. I'll have a car pick you up in front of your hotel."

"Great. I'll see you then."

Francis came back to the table.

"You look excited." Cassidy said.

"The guy from Washington wants another meeting. He stayed over just to talk to me. They are looking for a P.I."

"A private eye?"

"No. I'm sorry. That is a principal investigator. It's the lead scientist on a re-search project."

"You da man!"

"Not yet, but I think I have a shot at it."

"Let me guess, you are going off with him again, just when things are getting wet."

Francis didn't say anything. He fumbled with his napkin and looked every place except at Cassidy.

"Did I offend you, Francis?" Cassidy asked.

"No. Hell, no. It's just our timing really has a problem, doesn't it?"

"When are you meeting him?"

"Ten minutes."

"I see what you mean. Our timing is pretty bad so far."

Francis motioned for the waitress and the check. He picked it up and started to rise.

"Before you go, I have one more question for you." Cassidy leaned forward in her seat.

"Yes?"

"I want to know if you really think there is such a thing as healing water."

"Yes, I do. I think it needs help to be regenerated. This is the project I des-perately want to work on. I was disappointed last night when the water sample didn't turn out to be what I had hoped. I wanted to see the spring for myself, but Sanshi wouldn't take me there and now with the sample being so ordinary, I guess it was all just a big dream."

"You're practically sitting on top of it."

"What?"

"Sanshi, well, at least the one I talked to while you were off with who knows who, told me it was almost under the hotel."

"My Sanshi told me it was out of town a few miles."

"Sanshis Sanshis everywhere." Cassidy pretended to make a song.

"Where is it?"

"It's under the church."

"Damn, that makes sense. All the ancient churches in Europe and the Mid East were set on top of healing springs. That makes perfect sense. Well, who the hell did I talk to last night?"

"Hey, beats me. We went looking for you and my guy said he would come looking for you today."

"Listen, I've got to go meet with the Washington guy. If your Sanshi shows up, sit on him, tie him up, I don't care, seduce him if monks do that kind of thing, but don't let him leave until I get back."

"Fine. If he shows up I'll screw his top notch undone. Anything for you."

"No, I'm not…oh, you just got me there, didn't you?"

"We'll see. It's been a long dry spell."

"Come with me to the lobby?"

"Fine. I have to go to the local library anyway and look up sexual positions to shock a monk."

"Let it go, will you?"

Cassidy and Francis walked through the lobby. The Washington man was standing by a car in the circle drive outside. Francis opened the hotel door and turned toward Cassidy and gave her a hug with a brief kiss on the cheek. He turned away quickly and hurried to the car. Cassidy turned around to go to her room feeling a bit light-headed, lighter in spirit, and suddenly realized the car waiting for Francis was the same car that had carried away Sanshi, her Sanshi. She turned and burst out the door in time to see the car slipping down the hill and around the curve.

Chapter 9

"I'm pleased to talk to you again, Mister Purlough." Francis said as he sat down in the back seat of the car.

"Just call me Alford if that isn't too informal for you, Professor Allenton."

"Please, just call me Francis."

"Very well then, Francis. I want to get right down to business. I do have a plane out to Washington this afternoon from Springfield. We at the CAC have been interested in your research on the revitalization of water."

"I am flattered."

"The work you have begun shows promise. It relates highly to a project the CAC has set aside funds to investigate."

"I was unaware that the CAC had a grant-making program."

"This is a branch of the CAC you may not have heard about. We are interested in your results of water revitalization and are prepared to handsomely fund a project that has two areas of investigation. Are you interested?"

"Yes, sir. I am a bit surprised you know of my work in revitalization. It's a bit obscure and there was just the one article that came out last year."

"We are keenly interested in all research conducted about water and water vitality. The project we are going to fund looks at water revitalization and mineralization. As I understand your thesis, water can be revitalized using techniques first discovered by Schauberger. Is that correct?"

"Nearly so. Schauberger was not a researcher so much as he was a keen observer of nature and natural processes within water. He was a wild meister, loosely translated to English as a game warden. His fundamental notion that water is alive had Celtic roots. Fundamentally he felt the evidence for this belief was the spiraling nature of water, which he took as evidence of purposeful behavior. When he expanded his ideas beyond the Austrian rivers and ponds, he interpreted the current of the seas to be confirmation of his notions. He invented a number of purifying devices that relied upon spiraling and moving water and have subsequently been investigated. Those studies found that water gains a static electric charge as it tumbles or falls and, in particular, when it spirals."

"This led to the work by Schwenk?" Alford asked.

"Yes. Theodor Schwenk conducted studies of tap water moving through straight pipes versus water that had dynamic flow patterns. He demonstrated that naturally flowing water was more alive than straight pipe water, believing that water contained a natural proclivity to spiral because it had naturally occurring movement within it. Naturally emerging spring water, for instance, has been shown by the Schwenk's Institute for Flow Research at the University of Freiberg, to have distinctive flow and spiral patterns. When the water is slowed it loses its spiral movement and becomes stagnant and when subjected to spiral it becomes partially revitalized. Schwenk's Institute first suggested that water could be revitalized. My work is trying to move past those discoveries."

"You are using electromagnetic influences?"

"That's correct. The exact type and nature of these magnetic manipulations remain part of my development in the area. I do not have funds to conduct the level of experimentation I need."

"That may all change, if we can come to an agreement. Your study of ancient sacred sites around the world led you to use electromagnets. Isn't this correct?"

"Yes. I allude to this direction of research in the article. It is very astute of you to have concluded that my study of ancient sacred temples and ruins led me to the idea."

"Can you explain what you discovered at the ancient sites?"

"This is more conjecture than empirical evidence, but I am convinced that most neo-lithic sites were constructed above springs that were used for healing by ancient peoples. The function of the stone monoliths, such as are found at Stonehenge, is to use the naturally occurring crystal structures in the stones or perhaps naturally occurring magnets to amplify the curative aspects of the water spirals below them. Furthermore, the structures at Stonehenge are upright monoliths that were capped in such a way to make a complete circle. Now this might sound fantastic, and I currently have limited evidence to back this up, but I suspect the circular structure amplified the healing energy and produced a sort of healing environment highly charged with spiraling electrostatic energy. Some evidence exists, provided by a Welsh engineer Bill Lewis, that flowing water generates an electrical field that rises upward to the surface. Those who dowse for water use this electric field to locate water below ground in concert with the electromagnetic field generated by the dowser."

"Do you have any other similar findings?"

"Yes, sir, I do. Most sacred sites around the world are placed directly over underground streams or springs. Ancient beliefs gave water actual life or they associated certain springs and rivers with spirits. Pagans worshipped sacred springs. Notice I said worshipped the springs, not worshipped at the springs. In France a number of cathedrals, such as Chartres and Nimes, were built over springs that were previously sites of pagan worship. I'm certain you have heard of Lourdes. In England Carlisle and Glastonbury were built over sacred springs. Where we're standing now, Eureka Springs was built to capitalize on the healing springs that Native Americans used for healing and worship."

"It seems, Professor Allenton, that it cannot all be coincidence."

"Not to me. If you take into account the cradle of civilization was the Nile and India's holy river is the Ganges where people bathe not for hygienic cleanliness, but for spiritual cleansing, the picture begins to emerge: water has healing capacity. Many Buddhist temples have regular ceremonial ablutions. The Islamic traditions of certain purification rituals use water as a fundamental medium to bring new spiritual life. Many pagan beliefs were incorporated into Christianity such as baptism or the use of Holy Water. Christ declared himself to be the Living Water. When you consider the omnipresent myths across all cultures of the Great Flood and the spring of life in the Garden of Eden and Christianity's stories of Christ's walking on water and changing water into wine, the evidence is overwhelming, water in all cultures plays a predominant role in healing."

50

"And what have you found regarding the mineralization of water and the healing properties of certain minerals? As you say, even Eureka Springs arose from the healing waters taken by those who first visited here."

"Healing water has been a theme across all time. It seems that certain waters are charged with healing and others are simply water to nourish the body. Why certain waters heal and others do not is a mystery I hope to unravel. Ancient beliefs place an omphalos stone as a primary active agent in healing. The Celts and Saxons used ornate omphalos stones drawn from deep and sacred wells to carve the thrones of Kings. The spring and sacred stones at Delphi are just one example of the ability to tap into the turbulent nature of the planet and gain insight from the interaction. My own belief is that water passes through certain strata on the way to the surface. These substrata charge the water with healing energy, perhaps the electromagnetic charge in spiraling water releases mineral into soluble particles that change the fundamental characteristic of the water. Water thus charged may have the capacity to heal."

"An inspired notion, my dear Professor, inspired. But then, why do the springs lose their ability to heal?"

"That's the Nobel Prize question, isn't it?"

"Yes. I see what you mean."

"A phenomenological view would be that men have lost their belief in the ability of the water to heal them."

"You mean in the sense that people heal better and quicker if they believe in their doctor and his methods?"

"I mean that research has shown belief in healing promotes healing. I still maintain there is something to the chemical composition of the water that is unto itself healing."

"Yes, but then again evidence shows healing is as an act of faith."

"I do not dispute the psychological aspects of healing, but my research interest is in the chemical aspects of healing within certain waters. Once those natural waters have lost their ability to heal, it is my belief that such water can be revitalized using spiraling techniques and electromagnetic enhancement."

"This has been a most exciting discussion. I have one more area of discussion for you before I must leave. I want to know about your research on human behavior and mineral supplementation or deprivation."

"How much time do you have?"

"I know it is a difficult and arduous subject. If you would indulge me, I will show the relevance to our conversation."

The car had gone around the downtown shopping area loop. The narrow streets and various Victorian shops were no more than a blur to the otherwise focused men in the back seat. When their car pulled to a stop in the parking area across from the hotel's circular drive, Francis sank back into his seat. He crossed his right leg holding on to his foot with his left hand as if to anchor himself. His mind was racing to gather and somehow briefly produce the fundamental findings years of research had yielded concerning human behavior and minerals.

"Here is the broad stroke of it. I have a feeling you know most of this from our discussion the first time I met you, so I will just give you what I think are the most promising areas of development."

"Yes. I am familiar with most of this research. I am not interested in a literature review; I want to know your opinion of it."

"Some of it is flawed. It rests too much upon anecdotal evidence and not enough empirical studies with double blind subjects and methods. The studies in England, for instance, looked at violent youth and manipulated the mineral content of their drinking water. You know that it cannot be detected if manipulated at the angstrom level. The study was conducted in a prison and found some significant findings in the reduction of violence."

"So what is the problem you have with this study?"

"There are too many intervening variables. The inmates could have had access to illicit drugs, or if they were on drugs when they were incarcerated, their behavioral changes could be attributed to drying out. I just think the study was flawed."

"I'll give you that much. You do think that human behavior can be modified by minerals."

"Absolutely. We know that lead, manganese and other minerals will produce aggression and other chemicals will result in the production of serotonin and therefore have a sedating effect."

"The second aspect of our research program is related to the mineralization of drinking water for the military. The exact nature of the study is classified."

"The CAC is involved in military water experiments?"

"As I said, the study is classified. Professor Allenton, I can't tell you what a pleasure it has been. We will be in touch with you. How long will you remain in Eureka Springs?"

"I plan to leave tomorrow, but you can reach me by cell phone as you did today."

"Then we will be in touch with you by phone. I need to confer with my staff, but I feel confident in saying we are highly likely to make you an offer."

"I look forward to hearing from you."

Francis stepped out of the car. The interior of the car was darkened by tinted windows that also prevented anyone from seeing inside. Francis blinked and took a moment to adjust to the bright sunlight. He would try to find Cassidy and see if the monk had returned.

Chapter 10

Cassidy had stayed away from her room. She wandered around the hotel and went downstairs to a spa area. The feeling in the whole spa level made her uncomfortable. A shortness of breath came over her as she stood near the doorways that led to small rooms used for massage. Inside the waiting area a small boutique offered soothing elixirs and oils. Large crystals rested on window sills. They gathered sunshine that made rainbow designs on the walls.

She turned and retreated up the stairs. The housekeeper stood by the elevator.

"Hello again." She said as she passed by.

"Oh, hello. Did you find your boyfriend last night?"

"He's not really my boyfriend." Cassidy said.

Behind her Francis overheard the conversation. Walking up behind her he leaned close to her and whispered, "Hey, give me a chance."

The housekeeper laughed. Francis and Cassidy looked at each other and locking arms they strolled to the lounge area to sit on an overstuffed love seat.

"Whew! I'm bushed!" Francis let out a long sigh.

"You have the most interesting expressions. Do you ever wonder where things like that come from? I'm bushed?"

"No, not really. Do you?"

"Oh, yes. I find the mundane fascinating. Speaking of which, how did the water follies go?"

"Water follies? Oh, you mean the talk with Alford."

"Alford. There is a name that inspires confidence."

"He's quite educated, I'll have you know. He has read some of my articles."

"You can write?"

"You really are quite snotty at times, aren't you?"

"I have my reasons. So, really, how did it go?"

"They want me. That's my life story. Men of science want me, women don't."

"Don't be so sure of that."

"Really?"

Once again a silence came between them. Cassidy wondered what it would take for Francis to understand she was willing to make love to him. She had thought about it a lot when she was alone. She might be facing death or disfigurement and she wanted the attention of a man while she was still whole.

Francis thought about what Cassidy had just said. He knew he could be very assertive in the area of science, but was clumsy when it came to women. He had grown up interested more in his chemistry set than in the girls at school. He did not want to risk the embarrassment of coming across crude, but had made a fool of himself on several occasions with women. His last girlfriend devastated his self-confidence. Now he could tell the moment was dripping with anticipation for him to make the next move, but instead he asked, "Did the monk return?"

"You bet. I got him tied up in the room after I used every Kama Sutra position I knew on him. He's up there in a blissful place, one with the universe. Did you know that their peckers look just like little Buddha's?"

"Oh, come on, he never came back, did he?"

"No, good thing though, I was ready to hump him into tomorrow for you."

"Do you feel like having an adventure?"

"Boy, do I."

"Good. Let's go down – "

"Now you are talking." She interrupted him.

"As I was saying, let's go down to the church."

"Church? That's your idea of an adventure?"

"Come on, Cassidy. Let's go down to the church to see if we can find the opening to that spring your monk told you about."

Cassidy stood up. She looked at him directly. "You're not that bright about women are you?"

"Come on, let's go see if we can find it. It will be fun."

"Do men of science have children?"

"What are you on about now?" Francis knew he had upset her.

"You know what. This is the best offer I have had today. Why not? Let's go down there and see if we can discover the secret well of souls. You did see Indiana Jones didn't you?"

"Who?"

"For God's sake, you've got to get out more." Cassidy got up and went out the back door of the hotel.

Francis followed, but the door had closed and so he pushed. He pulled on the door and pushed once again. Cassidy watched him pushing and pulling and walked over to the double doors to open the other door, the unlocked door, for him. He smiled sheepishly at her and muttered his thanks.

Despite her frustration with him, she found herself liking him. He had a boyish smile and he could take her rapid fire sharp wit. He actually could give it back to her just as fast as she gave it. To her that meant he was bright.

They walked together toward the church's round tower structure with its green-shingled, domed roof. They passed the statue of Mary and followed the path by the little white plaster statues, the Stations of the Cross.

"They only gave Him vinegar, not water, to drink when he was dying." Francis said as they walked by.

Cassidy thought about what he had said but could not think of a response. She walked on and found a doorway in the back of the round stone tower. The door was standing open. A wheelbarrow beside it was empty and bags of cement and grout were piled on a wood pallet covered with a sheet of plastic. A shovel leaned against the building next to a bucket with a trowel and a sponge.

Cassidy went inside. She stuck her head back out and motioned to Francis to come in. The room was circular, as they expected, and in the middle of the room stood a stone altar. On top of the stone altar was a shallow, carved stone bowl.

"This is just like Sanshi told me." Cassidy said.

Francis approached the altar. Sun was streaming through a stained glass window. He could see the altar was attached to a large, circular stone base. He wrapped his arms around the stone and moved it to the side. A small opening could be seen below.

"Help me move this."

They pushed and slowly the opening grew. Ancient steps could be seen winding down to a spring that bubbled beneath them.

"I have to get a sample of that water."

"Go ahead. Who's stopping you? I'll stand guard."

Francis held on to the side of the stone floor and let himself down onto the first step. "It's slick down here." He whispered. "I can't see very well."

"Be careful." Cassidy called down to him.

"Damn!"

"What?"

"The water is five or six feet below where the steps stop. The water level has fallen all over this area due to over use. Damn! Can you come down here?"

"No!"

"Come on, Cassidy. I need your help to get some of this water. You should see this, the stairs make a near perfect helix. Perhaps it was used as an amplification chamber, like the ancient cathedrals and sacred pagan sites. There are drawings on the wall."

"What kind of drawings?"

"Strange things, fish, you know, like the ancient Christian symbol, and another one looks like a spiral universe, and there is a Caduceus, too. The water in the cistern is moving in a spiral pattern as it emerges from the spring. It's beautiful."

"Can't you just hang down from the step and get it?"

"No. I can't. I need you. I can hold your legs and you can get some for me."

"You're nuts. I'm not going down that hole, in the dark, so you can hold me upside down. What makes you think you can hold me?"

"How much do you weigh?"

"None of your business."

"Come on! Hurry up! Hell, what are you afraid of? You have already seen a ghost and lived through it. This might be what I have spent most of my life searching for. Come on, please."

"Not only no, shit no."

"What if I'm right? Come on, for me, your newest best friend. If you come down, I'll let you have some. Think about it! Perpetual youth! Perky young boobs your whole life? No wrinkles!"

"I'm thinking."

"Come on, Cassidy. I need your help."

"Will I fall in?"

"No. I got a great grip."

"Sure, all those years on the football team."

"Seriously, I won't let you fall. I have a collection jar in my jacket pocket. All you have to do is let me lower you over the edge. I'll pull you right back up."

"What if you drop me? I'll drown down there."

"I'll take off my belt and tie you to me. There is no way you will drop. I've done this before when I got samples at springs in Europe."

"What were the names of those dead people, the ones you left in the pools over there?"

"Come on!"

"Don't yell at me." Cassidy thought about it. What if the springs were healing springs like Sanshi said? What if they might offer her a chance at a cure? "All right. But so help me, if you let me fall or I get hurt, I'm going to get even with you. I'm a nurse and I know how to hurt you."

Cassidy held onto the side of the stones. Francis came back up and helped her lower herself down. When she reached the second step from the bottom, Francis took off his belt and put it around her waist.

"Watch my boobs, okay?"

"Yes. Don't worry. You'll be in and out in a second. Just hang over, take off the top of the beaker, and dip it in the water. Put the top back on and I'll pull you up."

Cassidy held tightly to the belt and let her upper body be lowered to the edge of the water. She collected the sample.

"OK. Francis, are you listening? Pull me up now."

Francis pulled on the belt and watched her legs which had remained partially on the last step. He leaned back to get leverage. She was strong, too, but it took both of them maneuvering to get her upright on the steps. The light from outside was growing dim. Francis put his belt back on while Cassidy took deep breaths. Then they quickly climbed up the steps and out of the hole. They pushed the stone back into place.

"You owe me big, mister." Cassidy was the first to speak.

"I can't thank you enough. Is there anything I can do for you?" Francis asked her.

"Yes."

"What? Anything."

"You can give me a sip of that water, and then you can make love to me."

Chapter 11

The World Health Organization headquarters had many divisions working in Washington. The CAC was a small division whose obscure office was rarely visited by outsiders. Alford Purlough arrived at the building and went straight to his office. His office was brightly lit and on three sides rows of bookshelves lined the walls with reports in labeled black notebooks as well as matched sets of official looking reference books. A conference table loomed large across one side near ceiling to floor windows. At the other end, two uncomfortable looking, straight backed settees flanked a corner, sharp-edged table. In the middle was his modest-sized desk. The phone was already ringing.

"Yes?" Alford was a man of few words.

"Mister Compton is here to see you," his secretary answered.

"Send him in."

Randal Compton arrived in a pin-striped suit. He had slid his tie open to make a lazy knot below his neck. He moved with certainty. He sat on a settee to face Alford and crossed his legs. His trousers pulled above his black socks revealing withered calves.

"What did he say? Is he our man?" Compton asked.

"We can get him."

"What project are we going to use?"

"Revitalization and mineralization."

"We don't have a lot of time. I'm going to Saudi the end of the week to negotiate the water deal. We need him committed by then. I need the infused water formula no later than a week after production gets started."

Purlough was scanning a report "How much are the Saudi's demanding?"

"Ten million, for now. All we need to do is be certain that the water for the troops is mineralized with the right formula. They won't care what we add to water we give our own troops, still, we need to be sure the plan is secure." Compton began to stand but instead shifted his weight, trying to find a comfortable place on the settee. The door opened and a highly decorated military man came in. Both men began to stand as he entered the room, but he waved them back into their seats.

"Gentlemen," was all he said.

"General, what's the status of the bottled water contracts?" Compton began.

"The commanders will go along with the restriction of only two bottles of water a day. We are attempting to justify the limits under cost cutting. Have your people dealt with the ROWPU's?"

Compton uncrossed his legs and shifted again. He faced the general and began to answer the question. "They taste like shit. We buggered the membranes so they would give off a nasty taste. Once the troops have had the bottled water, they won't touch that ROWPU crap. On top of that, we made sure the ROWPU's were delayed in shipping from stateside. Very few of them have been shipped."

"The uniforms are modified so the bottles fit exactly in the pockets." Purlough added.

Compton seemed to gloat, "The plan has been underway for sometime now. It is all fixed at this point. Ease of accessibility for the soldiers, ease of use, restricted amounts to concentrate the minerals, everything is going to plan."

"What about the Senate and White House?" the general asked Purlough.

"The bottled water in Arkansas is being adjusted as we speak. It won't taste one bit different."

"Are you certain?" the General asked.

"It has been the water supplied to the Senate and White House since Coolidge. They have confidence in the process, the safety and the purity. There won't be any questions.

"What are the consumption estimates for a war in Iraq?" Purlough asked.

"We are contracting for 9.5 million bottles a month. That's based on 160,000 troops each consuming two bottles per day."

"Who put the pressure on Paragonis?"

"Well, it was subtle. He did what he thought was right. He issued a press release about the contract with the Saudi's. The White House went for it, of course. The desalting plant is on line and ready to bottle. We will be controlling the mineralization in the final part of the process since it comes over to our people just before it is bottled. We got it locked up from there for security reasons. They went along with all of it. The last thing we have to do is a few bribes and we can start. Now I need reassurance about this water scientist you found. Can we trust this Allenton to get us the right formulation? Do you have Lin in place?"

"Yes, and Allenton will only be given partial information. I'll have the formula to start production." Alford had pushed his chair back and walked over to look out a window.

"So, you are confident the research is correct, that the minerals will produce aggression?" the general pushed the issue.

"Without question." Compton and Purlough said almost simultaneously.

"Dr. Allenton will think he is developing water that has healing properties for the troops in the event they are shot or are exposed to toxic chemicals? That's the research project I told him that we are funding." Purlough assured the general.

"Still planning to use manganese?" he asked.

"That's the best. Lead works better but is slightly more detectable."

"What about the civilian side?"

"We are working on the passivity side for the general water supply across America. We are going to be treating both the public treatment plants and the bottled water supply within the year." Compton continued to shift his weight. "Goddamn it, Alford, buy yourself a couch." He shot an angry glance at Purlough.

Purlough took no notice of his protest and continued to address the general. "Yes. We are working both sides. Bottled water consumption is at an all time

high. We have the local water plants on board under the guise of terrorism prevention and pro-active treatment agents being added to the water slowly and in
such a way as the general public won't realize the supply has been altered. The
minerals are trace elements and not easily detected. All water has minerals so
they won't be alarmed to find them in their analysis."

"We have certainly been successful in making the general public question
their tap water." Compton added. Have you seen the latest bottled water stats?
Use is going through the roof."

"How did you get the major players, you know, the soft drink makers on
board?"

"They are happy to comply with the new standards of mineralization. We
provided studies to show the minerals become as addicting as sugar or caffeine.
No one suspects anything. We will be manipulating most sources of domestic
water supplies, the municipal treatment plants and the bottled supplies, in a year
or less."

"So we've done it. It is truly coming together. We have the support of the
other countries. It has taken thirty years, but we have people in positions in
the G8. We have people on our payroll soon to be appointed as Sherpas. The
African members are giving us a problem. The upcoming conference in Evian
will be critical to our goals. We are pushing for a far-reaching water action plan
to emerge that will serve our political and financial interests. Following the
meeting in Evian our people in Washington are going to push for a Water Commission Act."

"Do we have the support of the environmentalists on the Water Commission
Act?" Compton asked Purlough.

"We have played our cards well with the environmentalists who will sponsor
the bill. Soon, the American public will be paying to help us reach our objectives. Appropriations have been suggested as high as eight or nine million per
year.

"Things are tracking along well. We will be making our recommendations
at the Sherpas' pre-conference in Evian, for a world water policy. The Africans
have tried to go outside the Sherpa system with personal representatives, but we
can work with it. We are assured by our insiders that the least we can hope for
in the Water Action Plan are several provisions within which we can continue
to work toward our objectives. The first area is the development of regulations,
institutions and technical frameworks for water policy development. The water
efficiency plans that we used in the United States will work in the other countries as well. We have hidden our agenda deep with the 'best practices' language.

"We are also pushing for a general clause for appropriate risk mitigation
mechanisms. We have found we can do much under that clause. We also intend
to push for a clause empowering local authorities as they are much easier to
bribe or manipulate. I think we can get funds again for research. They funded
the mineralization project for Allenton."

The general had approached a world globe on a stand by the windows. He
spun it and stopped the spin by placing a finger on Africa. "Africa is starting to

make some noise about the privatization of water. Once Europe and Asia agree to leave bottled water contents unregulated, we can begin the process in China. It is critical for our military objectives to control the Chinese water supply. Do you have Lin on board?"

Purlough turned toward him, "Yes. We arranged his defection last year. Once we start the privatization of Chinese water, the profits will be enormous. This is one of the largest emerging markets ever manipulated. Our people are projecting the success of our goals by 2011."

The general's voice grew louder, "We have to get the aggression formula in use so we can infuse the Saudi water. I want that formula and I want it last week."

"Allenton is close already. He has some other interesting ideas that will dovetail great with the cover." Purlough sat back down at his desk and began leafing through the contents of a manila file folder.

"So he's still intent on the healing waters?" Compton asked.

"That's his thing."

"What is that going to cost?"

"I think we'll get him and allow him to do his research for a total of a couple hundred thousand. Cheap by our standards."

"Do you think he was fooled by our imposter?" the general butted in.

"I can't say. We kept him from meeting the real Sanshi. I have Sanshi in a Federal detention facility under terrorism charges. He won't surface for ten years."

"I don't want Allenton near that original spring." Compton had grown emphatic.

"No problem. We will keep monitoring his e-mail and phone calls. When he comes on board with us we will have that locked down completely."

"That spring is the source water for the supply we are using at the White House and Senate. I can't afford to have anyone know its composition at the source. We are using lead there, aren't we?"

"It's a mineral that mimics the effects of lead only less detectable." Purlough answered.

"Allenton will be under constant surveillance then, when he comes on board."

"Pretty much like the rest of us."

"I'll talk to you tomorrow." Compton stood. He put his hands on Alford's desk. "We are too close now for any foulups." Turning, he let himself out the large oak door. It closed with a thud. The general gathered his brown leather briefcase and gave Alford a long and penetrating look. "I'll be in touch."

Alford took a bottle of water from a small refrigerator. He placed a filtering device on top of a cup and poured in the water. It dripped slowly as the filter removed all the minerals. Alford Purlough wouldn't be drinking what the rest of the world was.

Chapter 12

Cassidy and Francis pushed the stone back into place. He handed her the beaker full of the spring water she had collected in the cistern below the chapel.

"Just drink half of it." Francis instructed. "Before you drink it, swirl it around and around and make a slight vortex out of the water."

Cassidy unscrewed the top of the collection jar, swirled the contents around and around and drank the water. She wasn't positive, but she thought she felt sudden warmth throughout her body. She put the lid on tightly and handed it back to Francis. He placed it back in his inside coat pocket.

"Let's get out of here." He told her.

They walked in silence up the steep grade until they came to the stone gazebo structure with its alabaster white statue of the Virgin Mary. Francis pulled a cigarette from his jacket pocket and nervously lit the end. His hand was shaking. He looked at Cassidy and held eye contact with her.

"Well, I have fulfilled half my promise to you."

"Yes, you have."

"I'm a little awkward around women. Perhaps you noticed."

Cassidy tilted her head and gave him a coy smile. "Just a little."

"I'm not involved with anyone or anything like that. It's just that."

Cassidy interrupted him, "Don't talk yourself out of a perfectly lovely invitation. The less you say right now, the better. Just take my hand and take me back to my room."

"Perhaps we should go to my room?"

"Not on a bet. I couldn't get myself in the mood wondering if Theodora were watching."

"I can't really promise anything beyond today. You understand I am probably going to move to Washington to do research."

"You're talking again." Cassidy frowned at him.

"Yes. Yes. You're right. I talk when I'm anxious."

"There is nothing to be scared of. I'll be gentle with you. I'll only use half the Kama Sutra moves I used on Sanshi."

"I'm not scared or anything."

"Oh?"

"It's just my last experience was kind of devastating."

"I could lie in the bath tub full of water. That seems to arouse you."

"Don't you worry, you arouse me plenty all on your own."

"More talking. La, la, la, la." Cassidy put her fingers in her ears.

Francis stopped her from walking by placing his hand on her arm. She turned toward him and he kissed her deeply. He ran his hand up her side until he touched the outsides of her breast. Cassidy winced slightly.

"God! See! I'm sorry. I'm so clumsy."

"You are not clumsy at all. I'm just a little protective of that area. It's not your fault. You will never make a great discovery if you give up your research this easily. I'm not hurt. Try the other one."

They walked arm and arm into the hotel. He rang for the elevator. It seemed to take forever to arrive. When the doors opened, the car was between floors.

"After you." Cassidy teased.

They turned and took the stairs.

As they came down their hallway they could see the maid's cart outside the door to Cassidy's room. Cassidy looked in. The maid spoke first, "I'll just be a few more minutes." She smiled at them.

Cassidy and Francis looked at each other. They opened the door to Theodora's room. Francis kissed her deeply and pulled her inside with him. He pushed the door closed. All during the exchange of kisses and lovemaking Cassidy kept opening one or the other eye keeping watch for Theodora. She didn't come, but Cassidy did. Loud explosions of satisfaction rang out. The maid hurried down the hall giggling to herself.

Cassidy spoke first, "Damn. For a college man you ride like a cowboy."

"Thank you. I was pretty spectacular, wasn't I?"

"Modesty avoids you."

"Hey, let me have my moment. The last time I tried this I fell off."

"You're crazy." Cassidy hit him with a pillow.

"Is that why you like me, or is it my brain?"

"I don't know, haul it out again and let me take a look at it. That is what most men think with, isn't it?"

Francis scooped her up in his arms and they hugged. Both were satisfied in a way that they had not been for a long time.

"Get up and go in the bathroom, would you?" Cassidy asked. "I have to pee."

"Do you think we roused Theodora?" Francis got out of bed and went to the bathroom door. "I heard ghosts like to watch people make love."

"Go on. Who told you that?"

"I don't know. I think I read it somewhere. I have done a lot of reading about the occult."

"They must be jealous." Cassidy said. "Do you think there is sex in the afterlife?"

"It's my personal concept of heaven, all the sex and chocolate you want."

"Please, I really have to pee now."

Francis opened the bathroom door and went in. He let out a shriek.

"What?" Cassidy sat up in bed.

"I see a well-satisfied man in the mirror. I haven't seen one of these looking back at me in twenty years."

"Get out. I need to come in." Cassidy stood at the door. Francis put the towel over the mirror. "Good idea, you're such a clever fellow."

"Damn this room is cold. Can't they do something about it?" Francis put on his shirt and trousers.

Cassidy was warm and emerged from the bathroom nude. She felt comfortable with her shape and didn't need false modesty. She looked down at the small band aid on her breast from the biopsy three days ago.

Francis interrupted her thoughts, "Does it hurt?"

"It's nothing. Don't ask." Cassidy replied.

"Egad. I'm such an idiot. You told me that side was sensitive."

"I told you. It's nothing." She crawled under the covers.

A knock on the door startled both of them.

"Housekeeping!"

"Go away, we're screwing in here." Cassidy yelled out.

"Don't you ever censure yourself?" Francis asked.

"Life is short. I like to live in all four corners of the box life gave me. I work with death every day. You think you have a long time to live, but one day you wake up and you're facing the end of your life. I see people go through it and I go through it with them and their families. Everybody sees it differently. It is easy to be philosophical about death when it is someone else's."

"How do you manage to do the work?"

"I use dark humor and maybe more than a little bit of disrespect to the Almighty."

"I would have thought you would be trying to get a little bit closer to God if you worked in Hospice."

"God is a bully."

"What do you mean by that?"

"I mean that no one can withstand the will of God. He is like a bully on the play ground always getting his way. Somebody has to stand up to him once in a while."

"I don't think he is interested in a debate about his motives."

"You don't know that anymore than I do. You are an intelligent man and I'll bet nothing gets you going more than a good argument about what you believe or what are your intentions."

"Well, something got me going around here just a little while ago."

"You only promised me one roll in the hay."

"One good turn deserves another."

"The power of scientific persuasion melts my resistance."

"You already told the maid we were screwing in here. You wouldn't want to be a liar would you?" Francis teased and joined her under the covers.

This time their lovemaking was slow and deliberate. Cassidy thought it was delicious, but she could not shake the feeling that she had a strange burning inside.

When they had dressed she turned to him and in a matter of fact tone asked if she could ask him a question.

"Sure. What's the question?"

"I don't want to offend you, but do you have anything?"

"You mean like stocks and bonds?"

"No. I mean AID's or STD's?"

"Egad!"

"We are both grownups. We just had unprotected sex and I feel a burning sensation inside of me."

"Since when?"

"Actually, now that I think about it, since I drank the water."

"What kind of burning sensation?"

"It is very difficult to describe. I just feel warm all over like I might be coming down with something."

Francis put his hands in the air in a mock surrender. "Don't blame me. I'm pure as driven snow. You may not know this about scientists but they are obsessed with personal cleanliness and hygiene. I'm not offended. I would expect that kind of a question from a nurse. Perhaps it would be a better question before we made love, but none the less, that's a fair question."

"I didn't mean to offend you or anything. It's just a strange feeling. Perhaps from being hung upside down when we got the water sample and the blood rushed to my head."

"Perhaps it was my superior lovemaking."

"Yes, of course. What was I thinking?" Cassidy said in a sarcastic manner. "Not that there was anything wrong," she added to insure his pride would not be damaged.

"Seriously, are you feeling warm all over?"

"Seriously? Yes, I am."

Francis jumped from the bed and pulled out his field analysis kit. He took a small portion of the remaining water in the collection jar and put it in several test tubes. He lit a small burner under one and added some powdered material to the water. He shook the other tubes vigorously and then held them to the light for close examination.

"I can't really make a determination here, Cassidy, but this water shows signs of being vitalized or infused with certain minerals often associated with healing."

"Really?"

"Yes. I was hoping the water Sanshi told me about by e-mail would turn out to be this promising. I don't get it. Who the hell was the other guy, and why did they want to keep me from meeting with the real Sanshi? Get dressed."

"What?"

"Come on, get dressed. Let's go downtown and see if we can find that shop he told you about. Did you get an address?"

"How many Buddhist shops can there be?"

Chapter 13

Smells of incense greeted Francis and Cassidy as they opened the door to the shop and went inside. Wind chimes and a string of brass bells announced their arrival. A man came to the front of the shop.

"May I help you?"

"Is Sanshi here?" Francis asked.

"No. He is not." The man answered.

"When do you expect him?"

"I do not."

"I am a friend of his."

"He will be needing friends."

"What's happened?"

"He was taken away by people from the government last night. I cannot say why. They came this morning and told us he was with them and they also took his computer and some of his papers. They came into our home and took his things. They told us not to make inquires about him. They said it had to do with the 9/11 attack."

"Did they say anything else?"

"No. They said not to talk about it with anyone."

"Where was he taken?"

"They would not say."

"What was he charged with?"

"They would not say."

"Does he have any family or anyone we could contact?"

"No. When he chose the way of enlightenment, he stopped all contact with his former life. He lived alone and searched. He was a Tanha whose desires were born of ignorance, but he had become a Sotapanna, a searcher, entering the path to enlightenment. It is not possible for him to harm anyone or be part of any such plan. Such was not his way. Of late he spoke only of healing the sick saying he had found a great truth."

"Did the people who took him tell you who they were with? Did they show you any identification or badges?"

"Nothing. They acted as savages would act falling upon a wild beast. Sanshi is a tender man. He will not fare well in their prisons." The man turned toward Cassidy. "You have a strange light in you."

"I have a what?"

"You give off a strange light from within you. I have seen this light only once before."

Cassidy started to give a snappy answer to him but she found herself calmed by his sincerity.

Francis had pulled out a business card and gave it to the man. "If you hear anything at all, please call me."

"We shall not hear anything. I am certain."

"Just in case you do, call me."

Francis and Cassidy left the store. A short walk down the uneven stone sidewalk they found a bench. They sat and watched the traffic go down the street. Further down the hill a truck had started up but met an SUV. The vehicles were at a stand off. The woman in the SUV was waving her hand madly out her window at the truck driver. There was no place for him to turn or back down.

"What have you gotten yourself into, Francis?" Cassidy asked.

Before he could answer, the SUV started honking its horn. The truck was hauling cases of Arkansas bottled water. The driver emerged from his cab with a face red as a monkey's ass, and shouted at the woman. She slid down in her seat, rolled up her window, and reached up as if locking her door.

"Goddamn tourist! Where the fuck do you think I'm supposed to go?" the driver shouted. The woman sat up and started backing her car up the hill. She finally reached a space and backed into a parking spot.

The driver of the truck followed her and went to the passenger side of the SUV. He kicked the door causing it to buckle inward. The woman inside slunk further down the seat until only the top of her blond head could be seen. The man returned to his truck and gunning the motor sped up the hill. People on the street and sidewalks scattered in all directions.

"Have you noticed how many people have very short fuses?" Cassidy asked Francis.

Chapter 14

Francis packed his bags. He piled them in the hallway and knocked on the door across the hall. The door was ajar and it swung in slightly as he knocked.

"All ready?" Cassidy asked as he came in.

"Theodora has her room back. I'll bet she got an eye full yesterday."

"She's not the only one."

 Stiffness arose between them, the kind that comes from intensity followed by uncertainty.

"I'm not really good at good-bye." Francis said.

"Good. Me neither."

"Did the burning stop?"

"I feel much more like my old self this morning, thanks."

"I'm going to do a full analysis of the water when I get back to my lab. Who knows, maybe it's all true, what they say about the water."

"Who knows? Will you call me, about the water I mean?"

"Yeah. First thing, as soon as I know. You can call me, too, you know?"

"I know. Listen, about yesterday and all, I just wanted to say that lately I've been under a lot of pressure and..."

"Stop. It was wonderful. I'm glad you seduced me."

"Me? Seduce you?" Cassidy feigned the innocent voice of a little girl.

"Okay, it was mutual."

"Like hell, I practically had to bribe you."

They both laughed. Francis approached her. He moved close to kiss her. Cassidy held up her hand.

"Let's just leave it like this for now. Okay?"

"Yes. I see. That's probably better, isn't it, considering the circumstances."

He turned and picked up his suitcases. His arms full, he moved his head in a nod of goodbye. Cassidy returned the gesture. She felt suddenly sad, as if a ship were sailing and she was left behind. Francis walked down the hallway and turning gave her a boyish smile. He clunked his bags into the railings. Looking back, he shrugged, then disappeared down the stairway.

Cassidy turned back to her own bags. Most of them were packed and she was pushing on the largest one trying to make the metal closure fit into the slot. Her door slammed closed as if pushed by an angry hand.

"Theodora! Theodora, you listen to me. I mean you no harm. Leave me alone! I have enough trouble without you."

The bathroom faucet suddenly started to drip water. Grabbing her bags and pulling open the door, Cassidy fled down the hallway.

Chapter 15

Numbers 21: 9 Moses accordingly made a bronze serpent and mounted it on a pole and whenever anyone who had been bitten by a serpent looked at the bronze serpent, he recovered."

When Francis arrived at his lab in Columbia, his long time friend, fellow traveler and colleague Mark Hammond was waiting. "How did the speech go?" Mark asked.

"I kept a few of them awake."

"Oh, yeah? Well, Francis, I hate to hit you with this, but I've got bad news!"

"What?"

"They turned down the funding for the Caduceus."

"Didn't they read the report on the initial findings of the model?"

"We are talking about administration remember? What makes you think any of them can read?"

"What a bunch of fools. We are standing on the edge of a great discovery. Did they see the photos of the relic from the Temple of Aesclepius?"

"Palmeto thinks you are way off on this. His work on this is in direct conflict with an actual Caduceus, as you know, he and most of the world think the Caduceus is entirely symbolic."

"The evidence is staring them in the face if they could open their eyes and see past their own arrogance. Once the Caduceus has been conceptualized as only a symbol it loses all of its potential as an actual healing device."

Francis went to his bookshelf in the lab and pulled down a textbook. He flipped through the pages until he found a picture. "Look at this! This is as clear as can be. The Aesclepius Caduceus has only one spiral around a stick. The snake that winds around the stick is made of brass. See how the head of the snake is a larger diameter than the bottom. It just looks like a snake, but it is not in fact a real living snake. I think the Caduceus that was used by Aesclepius is the same one used by Moses. You know the Greeks used ancient artifacts in their healings. It is so clear to me. The model we constructed shows signs of electro-magnetic alterations in the basic structures of the water when it is poured into the mouth of the snake and winds its way down to the narrow exit. We know falling water gathers an electromagnetic charge as it falls, particularly if the water flows over iron ore material."

"Francis, you don't have to convince me. They think the Caduceus is a myth. They are not likely to change their mind."

"Didn't they read the attachments I sent? Couldn't they see the experiments I referenced? Didn't they take time to review the exact measurements of the artifact?"

"If they bothered to read it, they dismissed our ideas. Their interpretations of the Caduceus prevented them from seeing it any other way."

"How could they dismiss its origins? The Babylonian references are impeccable. The staff that Moses carried was from Ningizzida's site, I'm sure of that. It was a shepherd's crook. According to one source, part of it was broken off when he struck the Golden Calf with it. Later, when they wandered the desert and were plagued by snakes, he fashioned a brass serpent and mounted it to the staff. This is the same staff that Moses used as a dowsing rod to find water in the desert."

"That's if you take these accounts literally."

"The historical trail is solid. The Caduceus moves from Moses to Babylonia then to the Greeks, and then to the Romans. It was used by Galen and Hermes and eventually led the Druids and Celts to build serpent temples. The design was so successful it was copied throughout the old world."

"As I've said before, you don't have to convince me, Francis. I've always been on board with this. The Stonehenge sites and Asbury all have evidence of serpent cults. The committee is holding to the mythic interpretations when Aesclepius had a patient he could not cure and consulted a serpent. The serpent climbed the stick so they could talk face to face about what cures to use."

"So the committee would rather believe in a talking snake than an actual device based on archeological evidence?"

"No. They say the story is mythic like the snake in the Garden of Eden wrapped around the tree of knowledge. They see these as stories or allegories."

Francis paced about as if pleading with an invisible committee. "Well, they're half right. There's not a snake, but a brass device shaped like a snake and attached to a stick, usually olive wood, or a hematite rod, topped with a stone. What about the omphalos at the top of the staff? They can't deny the symbolism that the stone is a meteorite?"

"The object on top of the Caduceus has changed, depending on the text you consult. It has gone from a stone to a winged stone to a winged creature. The evidence is far from conclusive." Mark took on the role of the committee.

"Yes, yes. I'll give you that but look at the related evidence. The sacred stones had the capacity to change matter or at least have a profound ability to alter the matter it touched. This is a simple conceptual leap as far as I am concerned. The stone in the Egyptian rendering is obviously a meteorite. This is the oldest known depiction of a Caduceus. Later renderings show the stone with wings, obviously a reference to its origin from space. Rocks don't have wings."

"As you say, the only rocks that fly are meteorites, but – " Mark continued.

"The black meteorite in the Holy Shrine in Mecca, most likely a Gray Hematite crystal, is the stone that Mohammed supposedly touched. The long lived legend of the philosopher's stone was most likely a hematite as well. Recent evidence from images that are able to detect the chemical composition of stones indicated that Mars has vast regions of gray hematite. There has been a long standing belief that life on earth may have been seeded by a meteorite from Mars or some other nearby planet. When such a meteorite came into contact with Earth's atmosphere it would have exploded and sent smaller meteors all over the world. All these sources point the way to a stone that has the ability to concentrate energy and alter the fundamental characteristics of everything it touches. How can all of this research be denied?"

"Yes. I agree, but that is their decision and I really don't see anything we can do about it."

"It's has been there, right in our faces, all these years: the Hippocratic Oath and the ever-present Caduceus on medical degrees and nurses' uniforms. They're all a carry-over from the time when every ancient healer had a Caduceus through which he would pour water and use that water to heal the sick. If it isn't true, why has the symbol endured over time and across so many cultures?"

"Francis, they say it's because it is a symbol."

Francis picked up a stack of papers, "Look at these. The report on the electromagnetic anomalies when the core is hematite or iron ore and direct current electricity is applied. The report where the Caduceus device actually levitates when pulsed with microwaves. The reports of strange magnetic field disturbances that defy electromagnetic theory and the loss of time, are all here. Rather than have a single resonance of electronic field, the device has infinite resonance seemingly able to fix itself to any nearby frequency. In so much as every living person has their own unique magnetic field signature, the energized Caduceus could align itself with each person placed before it so the healing would be perfectly matched in resonance and electric field. I'm telling you, Mark, I am right about this. I will not accept this as a life of research gone to waste"

"We could appeal again." Mark offered.

Francis picked up the rest of his submitted research papers on the Caduceus and turning around dropped them in a bottom file drawer. He paced around the lab. Suddenly he stopped and pulled up a lab stool directly in front of his friend and fellow researcher and sat facing him, "Mark, how attached are you to Columbia?"

"Well, Mary and the kids are pretty well settled. I suppose we could move if we had to. Why?"

"I may have an opportunity outside in government work. If it works out, I will want you with me. There will be plenty of money for whatever we want. No more of this petty crap going through egos and committees."

"Francis, you've obviously never worked for the government."

"No, I haven't, but it's got to be better than this department. I've wasted my talents here and so have you. I expect to hear more any day now." Francis got up and walked over to look out a window.

Mark was quiet for a few minutes then spoke, "A package was delivered this morning for you." He lifted a white package from Francis' desk

Francis looked at the return address: World Health Organization Collaboration Center at New York University.

Mark's finger was resting on the logo of the W.H.O., a single serpent Caduceus. He looked up to see Francis also staring at the Caduceus. "Well, open it!"

Francis tore open the envelope and began to read a letter to himself. About half way down he crossed his arms and pulled the letter to his chest.

"Yes. This is it. My God! I've been waiting for this my whole life. It's a research project and they want me as principal investigator. They tell me to select my own staff and report to New York within twenty days or they will withdraw the offer. My salary will be doubled and there is relocation money, lab money and a generous allowance for outfitting the lab. All right, Mark, this is it, I'm going to New York."

Mark stood staring at him.

"Mark, this is for you, too, come with me. This is the move we've been waiting for."

"Wow, Frank, first I'll have to talk to Mary. But unless there is something I haven't thought of, I'm in, yes, definitely, I'm going with you to New York."

"Great. Now I have to call someone." Francis said.

"Call who?" Mark asked.

"I met someone at the conference."

"You got lucky?"

"Yes, very lucky, twice in one day."

"Well, when you're hot, you're hot."

"Yes, sir, life is good today. Will you do me a favor? Set up the analysis for a sample I brought back."

"Sure thing, give me a moment."

Mark started to set up the analysis materials and experiments for the sample. Francis really wanted to call Cassidy right away with the news about the new contract and the move to New York, but he decided to wait until the lab results were completed. He walked over to a locked cabinet and removed the Caduceus model that Mark and he had built. He held in his hand a single brass spiraling coil with an opening at the top larger than the bottom. The spiraling coil was wrapped around a hematite core. He had selected the hematite because of its strong magnetic potential. Electric connectors had been braised to the brass coil so direct current could be applied as water was poured through it. At the top of the Caduceus' core was an opening that awaited a stone. The cost of a meteorite was beyond their budget at this point.

The end of the coil was smaller in diameter than the head so the water would be accelerated as it fell through the coils. He took a small portion of the water from Sanshi's spring and sent it through the spiral. The water was collected in a small beaker as it emerged. Mark then began the comparison between the spring water from the jar and the spiraled spring water in the beaker.

Francis decided he couldn't wait any longer. He picked up the phone and called Cassidy.

Chapter 16

The telephone rang three times.

"Hospice of the Ozarks," a pleasant voice answered.

"Cassidy Martin, please! It's urgent."

Dreadful programmed music came on the line as Francis was placed on hold. He shook his head as if he was attempting to shake the noxious rhythm out of it.

"Nurse Martin. May I help you?"

"Cassidy, it's Francis."

"You did call. My faith in mankind has been restored."

"The World Health Organization wants me."

"I told them all about your prodigious skills as a lover. Of course they want you now."

"Seriously, I'm going to New York."

"New York? That's funny."

"Funny, how?"

"I'm going to New York early next month. I have a meeting there."

"God, that's great. When? Where?"

"Sloan-Kettering."

"You're job hunting?"

"No."

"What do you mean? Is it a conference?"

"No."

"Come on, Cassidy. I never knew you to be so quiet. Why are you going there?"

"Sloan-Kettering. Ever heard of them?"

"Yes, of course, the cancer center."

Silence once again filled the space between Francis and Cassidy. Francis let the realization of what Cassidy was telling him sink in. He found it hard to find words.

Cassidy finally spoke. "Maybe we could do lunch or something."

"Yeah. Cassidy, oh my, give me a minute, I'm just putting some things together here."

"Such a clever boy."

Taking the phone away from his ear, Francis lightly banged the end of the receiver against his forehead then took a deep breath. He brushed his tongue against his upper lip, and putting the phone back to his ear, said, "Not so clever apparently."

"Don't be too hard on yourself."

"Is there anything I can do?" Francis asked.

"Yes. Don't change how you treat me one bit, and, Francis, there is one more thing."

"Yes?"

"Let me know if that damned water will fix me."

"Belief in the water and the ability to be cured is part of it, you know, it's a big part of it."

"Well, I'm screwed then, aren't I?"

"I need to talk to you, Cassidy. I'll come down there."

"There you go, changing our agreement already. I don't do pity very well."

"Cassidy, I don't have the water results yet. We're just now running a comparison test. I will know something later today, however."

"Then I'll hear from you later today."

"Yes, definitely later today."

"Good bye, Francis."

"Cassidy, yes, later today. Good bye."

Francis held the phone a while after the line had gone dead, remembering what it was like to hold Cassidy. Mark was busy in the lab, but looked up and noticed Francis cradling the phone.

"You all right, Francis?"

"I suddenly understand why I went into chemistry. After I dropped out of medical school, I still wanted to cure people. I just looked at it as an intellectual curiosity most of my life. Now I understand why people have searched so hard to find a cure for disease and illness. I get it. Finally and for once I get it."

"What's going on, Francis?" Mark turned to look at him.

"The young lady I met in Eureka Springs has cancer."

"Is it bad?"

"It is cancer, isn't it? Oh, God, I went on and on about water and the healing springs and all the shit I preach and she just stood there and took it. No wonder she was so interested in the springs. I feel like a perfect fool."

"How were you to know, Francis? You're too hard on yourself."

"That's what she said. No, no I'm not, but I did let her drink some of the water she helped me collect at the hidden spring. She said it made her feel warm inside. I thought maybe it was the mineral content or something. I've led this girl on. Her life is in peril and I'm talking bullshit to her about healing."

"But you believe it has happened, that water has healed people in certain circumstances. You don't know that your experiments with revitalization won't activate some healing combination of circumstances or events."

"That's all very good and well as an academic argument. It is fine for me to spend my life looking for a piece of a puzzle, but this young woman can't wait for the puzzle to fall into place for her. Mark, we have to redouble our efforts. We have to press on, take some chances and do something for her directly. It's not a publication or a Nobel Prize anymore. This is life and death and it is the life and death of someone who I happen to really like. There must be something more, something I have missed. It can't be that I have found this path that leads across history only to come up short the first time it really could do some good. Let's get back to that sample I brought you and take a look at it now that I have spun part of it through the Caduceus machine."

"Francis, it's been through the analyzer already. I'll print out the results."

Mark busied himself with the computer printout of the water sample analysis.

Francis realized that all the time he had been talking he had been clutching the phone "Don't you worry, little lady, don't you worry. I've got some tricks up my sleeve." He slowly placed the phone back on the receiver.

Francis walked to his bookshelf and pushed aside recent textbooks until he found the one he wanted. Carefully dusting off the jacket, he opened to the title page, *The Effects of Water, Cold and Warm, as a Remedy in Fever and Other Diseases*, James Currier, Scottish physician and surgeon, 1797. He had read the book a hundred times.

Francis turned on a light at his desk and sat down leafing through the yellowed pages.

"Back to Currier?" Mark asked.

"There's something here, Mark. I know it. I can feel it. All these studies on water and the interactivity of water with human energy are trying to tell me something."

"That area of inquiry is what earned you your reputation as an eccentric. I thought we agreed it would be better if you just let it go."

"I need to review this one more time. Did you ever work and work on a math problem in school before you understood how math worked and suddenly you got it?"

"Well, sure, sometimes when I was first starting with math."

"You know how you could make the numbers work, but the elegance of the formula or how the process worked would escape you until it just hit you and then all the problems could be solved. You have to catch the essence of the process in your mind and the way you did it was problem after problem. While you are learning, it's just a bunch of numbers to put together and you hope you get it right, but once you see the formula and incorporate it into how you think about the numbers, they all fall into place. That's how I feel about all these studies about water. I can't quite put it together, but I know the answer is staring back at me.

"Mark, it's like Currier is staring at me. He saw something elegant in how minerals are active in nerve transmission, cell permeability, tissue formation, and healing. Over two hundred years ago he saw what some water scientists are just now coming to realize, water is the key structure to body health and disease prevention and healing. The ancients knew that water was alive, but, not really understanding the nature of water, they attributed the sense of life to deities or spirits that lived within the water. Now we have to consider the research about memory in water."

"Now, Francis, you know that's a very subjective study," Mark spoke with a distinct tone of skepticism.

"I'll give you that, Mark, but what if it is true? What if we could determine that water has a kind of memory capacity? Fifty years ago people would have laughed if you would have told them that silicate sand could have a memory and now it is the primary substance used in memory boards for computers. On one level it is only sand, on another level, it has memory and now it seems, it can learn. Once electricity was introduced to chips made of silicate, they began to show the possibility of structural manipulation that allowed them to be manufactured on the microtechnology level."

"Because something has memory, does not mean it is alive."

"There is a long held belief in certain cultures that water has a kind of consciousness and responds to human interaction. Tibetan monks still chant regularly around the community water supply. They believe that water thus energized assists the villagers in the cure of physical ailments. I know I'm on to something, Mark. We need to take another look at Schweitzer's study. You know, David Schweitzer, Albert Schweitzer's grandson, doesn't that give him some credibility? He's the one who photographed the effects of human thoughts in water. His photographs demonstrated that water acts as a liquid memory system. Computers of the future might be made of energized water. Perhaps nanotechnology will manipulate water with curing memory and when you drink the water it will seek out germs and impurities in your tissue and remove them"

"Okay, Francis, then what about that Canadian experiment where water enriched with antibodies had the antibodies filtered out and the water retained the curative power?" Mark asked.

"Yes, yes. I don't know how it all comes together yet. I can tell you we are close with our present line of research."

"Is this what the World Health Organization is funding, research on healing waters?"

"No. The group is a small division within the larger organization. They have only given me the broad picture, the rest is classified. I'm not certain, but by the questions they asked me, I think it has to do with mineralization in order to bring about desired behavioral changes and also prevention. Something about how the water for military troops might be fortified to decrease the chances of infection if they are wounded."

"That's bloody brilliant. Our guys will be drinking water that immunizes them against infections when they get wounded. I love that idea." Mark added.

"They want to fund our experiments on water revitalization and look at healing springs' potentiality. I'm sure of that much anyway."

"So, what of the behavior manipulations?"

"I don't know, Mark, I'm in the dark on that one. The lab is housed in their Collaborative Center which is primarily an arm of their psychiatric health efforts. We will just have to wait until we are on board."

"Hey, Francis, do you have anything that might get in the way of a top secret security clearance?"

"I don't know. How far back do they look?"

"Well, I really don't know. What do you have to worry about?"

"Oh," Francis smiled, "just the same things everybody else did growing up in the seventies. No big deal. Well, this packet here has a set of forms for me to fill out. I'll make a copy for you, too."

Mark went back to the computer analyzer. The results for the water sample from Eureka Springs were being printed out.

"Holy Shit, Francis. Come here and take a look at this."

Chapter 17

Alford Purlough hurried to the meeting. The secure elevator required both a card and voice recognition. Millions of dollars had been spent over several decades and as the water cartel approached a major milestone in their planning, Alford had been summoned to give a report.

Entering the meeting room, Purlough noticed the secretary's efforts to warm up the sparsely furnished room with a colorful spray of flowers on the long, conference table. In the corner was a large bottle of water with a complex filter attached to the spigot. Members of the water cartel began to arrive. Following some handshaking and storytelling, the meeting began.

Alford approached the podium. A slender spotlight lit the pages in front of him. He began, cleared his throat, and started again.

"The services of Doctor Francis Allenton have been secured. Under a cover of the World Health Organization's C.A.C. branch, employment has been successful. Our plan and the plans of some of our fathers, to alter the mood of the Senate and White House with mineralized water, have begun. We will soon have a suitable formula.

"Under the guise of the spread democracy around the globe, we continue to move forward. When the war is officially started in the arid regions and the Armed Forces of the United States are placed there for a prolonged period of time, vast amounts of bottled water will be needed. From our calculations, a standing force of over 160,000 men would consume nine and a half million bottles of water per month. This water will be provided by selected members of the group with financial interests in bottled water franchises. When you add this to our other global water efforts, profits will reach nearly twenty billion dollars a year."

The men and women gathered around the table nodded to express their pleasure with Alford's report.

He continued. "On the domestic front, the water cartel has been successful in planting a seed of doubt in consumers' minds about the safety of tap water. Over the last several years we have managed to manipulate water figures to encourage state, community and municipal restrictions on water use and drive up the demand for bottled water. We have timed the placement of a wide variety of choices of bottled water on the shelves of supermarkets and in vending machines to stimulate purchases. Simultaneously, we have been able to defeat any efforts to regulate the contents of bottled water and thus many of our products are packaged tap water, selling at a premium of nearly one thousand times more than the cost of production.

"Our water cartel has completed the plans made by our predecessors in the fifties when Eisenhower had his heart attack. The White House has stocked and used water from Arkansas since those times. Recently, we gradually have begun to add minerals to the water supply at the bottling plant. These minerals will produce aggression and thus the winds of war will be easily fanned.

"Now with the prospects of war in the Mid East following the 9/11 attacks, the time is right for our largest and most ambitious plan. We already have been successful in replacing the ROWPU's with bottled water. That water will be manipulated to increase the aggression in the men and women of the Armed Forces. The military was quick to sign on to provide bottled water for soldiers believing that bottled water will improve morale when troops are deployed to arid regions.

"The plan is working flawlessly. Since the 2000 election has gone our way, and the aggressive mood in the Senate is increasing, the possibility of a protracted war in the Middle East is almost certain. The only challenge that remains is perfecting the formula that will significantly increase aggression in the troops. War produces its own aggression, but a formula is needed that will insure troops will act savagely and in some instances, irrationally in combat situations. The anticipated resistance of the insurgency, as some will call it, hardly needs to be fueled by aggressive minerals, but, we are taking no chances. Thus, our plan calls for the immediate destruction of the entire Iraq water supply and infrastructure. Our military members have assured me that the infrastructure will be damaged beyond repair once the war officially starts. Of course, our companies are positioned to rebuild those plants and produce bottled water or treated water to our specifications."

One of the cartel members raised his hand.

"Yes?" Alford acknowledged the hand in the air.

"Where are we with the additional brewing companies and soft drink manufacturers?" the man asked.

"I have a meeting with some of them today."

As soon as the meeting was over, Alford took the secure elevator to the first floor and got in his limousine. As they started to his office, his secretary called, "The gentlemen from the brewing concern are here to see you. Are you almost here?"

"Yes, I'll be there in five. Show them in."

When he arrived he found a tall man, impeccably dressed in a pin-striped suit, sitting across from a smaller, balding, dark-haired man, attired in a custom-made suit. Alford knew they were interested in joining the water cartel, but he also had been told they would be pressing for market exclusivity.

The two men stood. "Gentlemen, please sit down. Do let me take a moment to explain a few of the facts about the future of water as I see it. Water promises to be to the 21st century what oil was to the 20th century. This will be the substance that determines the wealth of nations and the wealth and power of those who own it. Fresh water represents less than one percent of the world's total water supply. The population explosion is adding 85 million people every year while the use of water is doubling every ten years. *Fortune Magazine* has estimated the annual profits of the water industry will soon reach 40 percent of those of the oil sector. This is substantially higher than the pharmaceutical sector. We anticipate close to 1 trillion dollars of business by the year 2004.

"Since our present cartel was formed, there have been more than $15 billion worth of water acquisitions in the US water industry alone. The World Bank predicts that water will soon be moved around the world as oil is now. We stand for the privatization of water and that means the management of water resources will be based on principles of scarcity and profit maximization rather than long-term sustainability. Corporations must invest in the use of chemical technology, desalination, marketing and water trading to insure their share of the market. Conservation will soon be relegated to fringe elements. We are making aggressive efforts to identify environmentalists as crackpots. We will be pouring millions of dollars into the next election to ensure free market perspectives and increased deregulation will be the mark of progressive politics."

Alford watched their demeanor as he spoke. They seemed to be in agreement. "Well, gentlemen, the time for decision is upon you. We need to know if you are in or not."

The taller man spoke, "Mr. Purlough, we are definitely in. We thought this was clear by our sizable donation to the foundation this year. We can't afford to let anyone else in the industry corner the water market. However, as we clarified earlier, we cannot have any exposure at this time. We must be invisible partners."

"Very good, I'll have my men draw up the papers. Where are you staying?"

"We are at the Plaza."

"I'll have a few of my associates come around to see you tonight. I think you will find them most entertaining."

"Certainly, reports of your social contacts are legendary, Mister Purlough."

"The girls will be around to your rooms around ten tonight."

"As always, Mister Purlough, it is a pleasure to do business with you. We are expecting exclusive rights."

"Gentlemen, we simply cannot do that. We will have several dummy companies between you and the water distribution companies. As I said before, there are others involved, well-placed people in companies with existing contracts with the Government, and we cannot tamper with them."

The two men looked at each other. The tall man stood and walked to the window.

"Mister Purlough, this venture represents a significant investment on our part. We need exclusivity in the contract."

"I mean no disrespect to you and your company. However, you have neither the means nor capital to be our exclusive partners. I'm not certain you understand the scope of our interests. The Government contract alone will mean nine, perhaps ten million bottles per month. We can't delay our contracts and wait for you to tool up to that level. Perhaps in a year or so we can begin to slide more work in your direction. Right now it is too large to put in one place without arousing suspicion."

The men looked at each other. The smaller man pushed a brief case toward Alford. "Perhaps this small token of appreciation will move the contracts toward us sooner than later."

"Perhaps. May I assume you are in?"

"Yes, Mister Purlough, we are in. There was some mention of a formula."

"Yes. We will have some expectations of purity and mineral content. Our people will get with yours to work out the formula for the mineralization. Our extensive research shows the minerals at trace levels will result in dependency patterns similar to those found in many of your cola products."

"Are there any consequences as far as taste?"

"Not one bit. The alterations will be tasteless. It is a condition of your participation. I was led to understand you were aware of this?"

"We don't have a problem with this expectation."

Alford stood and shook hands with the men. "This concludes our meeting then. I'll have the papers brought to you later tomorrow. Gentlemen, enjoy your evening."

Chapter 18

"Welcome to New York, Francis."

"It's nice to see you, Mister Purlough ."

"Have you been through the lab?" Purlough asked.

"Yes. It seems quite adequate. I was wondering about the approval of my assistant?"

"We are processing his request for security clearance as we speak. Did you meet the other people at the lab?"

"Yes. They all seem highly competent. I was wondering if you got my message about the revitalization equipment."

"Yes. I'm not certain I understand the request. You want copper tubes in decreasing diameter and a ferrite core seven feet by seven inches. Is that right?"

"Yes, sir. This is part of the revitalization process we talked about. I would like to begin my work on this right away."

"I'm certain this will be reviewed. Until such time as I have final approval on this request, I want you to begin immediately with the mineralization experiments."

"I read the prospectus on this. This is a fascinating direction, the reduction of aggression through the use of mineralization of the water."

"We will need a preliminary report in two weeks. We want trials in both directions, both mineralization that increases aggression and mineralization that decreases aggression for a comparison study. We have secured volunteers for the trials."

"I'll get started right away. You are aware, however, that my primary interest is in the other research area, the healing water area."

"We are aware of your interests in this area. The first priority, however, is the mineralization project. Are you going to follow your primary methods, the neurotransmitters?"

"Yes, the release of excitatory neurotransmitters can be triggered by some of the minerals in question. These same minerals will interfere with the absorption of dopamine and thus the entire nervous system will become agitated. I am focusing first on manganese."

"Excellent. I'll need to see results on this right away. As I understand your methods, you have to confirm the agitation effects and begin removing minerals until you isolate the ones that bring about the agitation."

"You're a quick study, Mister Purlough. That is the best method, but I have a concern that the water might retain the capacity once the minerals are removed."

"You don't hold to that intelligent water nonsense, do you?"

"I hold to anything I can't disprove. The Canadian studies showed water's ability to retain healing properties when antibiotics were introduced and then filtered out."

"You do have the reputation of an eccentric, a brilliant one, but none the less, an eccentric."

"Perhaps, if you knew my true character, you would not have brought me on board as the principal investigator."

"You would be surprised how much I know about you, Francis. You are exactly the man I want on this project. Your interest in revitalization and the ancients hasn't escaped my attention, nor has your model Caduceus. It does seem a rather fanciful expenditure. I have seen your request for materials to reconstruct the artifact discovered in Greece. Are you still confident the expense is worth it?"

"This is no eccentricity, Mister Purlough. The evidence is strong that the Caduceus is not a symbol but an actual device for healing. There are references throughout history of a healing vessel. The descriptions vary somewhat. I have made my life's work the discovery and authentication of the Caduceus."

"I continue to need some convincing, Francis."

"Let's go back to the reports of King Solomon commanding the spirits of healing that emanated from a vessel of brass. The brass container had the rough shape of a Caduceus."

"Once again this may have been a story to promote his status as a king. The bowl or vessel of healing may only be symbolic."

"Think about it for a moment. In order for a symbol to endure and be shared across cultures, some particle of truth must exist. Symbols that endure are not arbitrary in any way; they strike a resonance within the human spirit and are maintained and elaborated across time. There are very few symbols as enduring as the Caduceus. One method to verify the power of a symbol is for that symbol to endure across time and across cultural lines."

"Equally enduring in many cultures is the symbol of the serpent. Are we to suppose that there was an actually talking serpent in the Garden of Eden?"

"Religious symbols may be grounded in fact as much as pagan symbols. I canot say, nor can any person say, that there was a serpent that tempted Eve in the Garden, but the portrayal of the serpent as a phallic or healing symbol crosses many cultural and religious lines. There are numerous historical manifestations of the serpent related to healing or rebirth, such as the ouroboros, the self-consuming serpent."

Francis drew a breath, "Then, also, we can look at an actual cup of bronze made for the King of Lagash in 2000 B.C. found in Sumerian and must ask ourselves, was the cup ceremonial and used in healing practices to inspire faith in the person being healed, or did the cup have healing properties? This cup is the first known artifact where the spiral and the Axis Mundey cross at seven principal points."

"The Axis Mundey being a form repeated throughout history as well?" Purlough asked trying to keep pace as Francis became more and more excited.

"The primary form of six points merging at the seventh has religious meaning and actual confirmation as a life-giving and life-defining shape. Not only is the motif found in ancient European artifacts, the Aztecs used the double entwined serpent in their religious and healing iconography. They had two feathered serpents wrapped around a shaft to indicate healing energy. Again, the coils are crossed into seven nodal points.

"These shapes are used to represent the God of healing in so many cultures it cannot be coincidence. Take the Kindling Yoga belief of coiled serpent power. They describe the substances of the body as consisting of the actual body and the energy of the body. The image is that of two coils of energy wrapped around the spine. These coiled filaments, one feminine and one masculine, cross exactly at seven nodal points. These points, or chakras, are used as maps to healing."

"Like DNA?" Purlough attempted to slow Francis down.

"No! Not like DNA but actual DNA. These representations by the ancients are the equivalents of DNA. Perhaps there is some kind of spiritual self-awareness on the molecular level or perhaps the form is present because it is a substantial form of life seen and confirmed as a sacred shape, I don't know. In 1953 when Watson and Crick discovered the structure of DNA, it was a spiraling double helix. It is not represented symbolically as a double helix. DNA is an actual double helix. DNA is not a symbol of life and regeneration. It is life and regeneration. DNA is the same shape that has dominated the description of healing throughout ancient times. Coincidence, Mister Purlough?"

"It does seem unlikely." Purlough was keeping pace.

"Nor can it be explained that the DNA molecule consists of six elements that are joined by the essential seventh component, the spine of hydrogen bonds spiraling into a single molecule of life. Not symbolic of life, Mister Purlough, but actual life that is repeated all around us, across time and cultures and into space. Our very galaxy is a spiral galaxy and perhaps all life sprang from that spiral. It takes very little imagination to look at the model of DNA and see the undulating serpents around a core.

"I tell you, Mister Purlough, it is maddening. I have perhaps a deserved reputation for being eccentric. I know I have seen a great truth, but the exact meaning and value of this truth eludes me. I cannot seem to turn my mind away from it."

"So it is with many great truths, Doctor Allenton, they lie just outside our grasp."

"With every ending comes a new beginning compelled by a will beyond knowing." Francis said the expression aloud with his eyes closed.

"Something you read once?" Purlough asked.

"No. A Buddhist Monk in Eureka Springs sent it to me by e-mail."

Chapter 19

Francis had called Cassidy back as he promised, but he had decided to reserve his water analysis results for when he saw her in person. Shortly after his call, she called him with the confirmation of her appointment at Sloan-Kettering for treatment. She told him that her cancer had initially gone into a recession but now had reemerged more virulent than before.

Francis offered to pick her up at the airport, and now, while he waited for her in the baggage area, he wondered if she had changed. How would she look? What would he say?

Then he saw her and as he started walking toward her, he called out, "Hey, Cassidy, how are you doing?"

"Hey, Francis, I'm great. Doesn't it look that way?" Cassidy waved her arm to greet him.

As she came closer, he could see that her gait seemed slower, more labored, and her high energy persona had withered some.

"Like I said, how are you doing?" Francis reached out to hug her.

Cassidy gave a quick hug and turned toward the baggage area, "I have good days and bad days." She turned back, "Okay, Francis, enough about me, how is your job going?"

"It is great, really. They give me all the room I need to work and everything I ask for shows up eventually. I am getting a major piece of equipment assembled today for the regeneration experiment."

"I'm truly happy for you." Cassidy said as she walked to an overnight bag and got it off the carousel.

Francis moved forward, "Let me get that for you."

"Keep your hands to yourself. Remember, you promised not to treat me differently now."

"I was nice to you before, remember?" Francis said in defense. "Seen any ghosts lately?"

"Only when I look in the mirror," she replied.

The double meaning didn't escape Francis' attention. He felt the awkward silence emerge between them that seemed to be a hallmark of their relationship. He pushed himself to keep talking. "The results on the water sample we took were initially very interesting. I had hoped it might have helped you."

"Actually, I felt much better for a week or two. You remember my friend, Doctor Dean? She was encouraged by the results in the first two weeks, but it came back twice as mean and has been kicking my ass since then. I don't suppose you have found a cure for me yet?"

"Not yet."

"Well, you better get with it. Clock's ticking you know."

"I know. Well, I do have an idea. It's a little off the wall."

"I'm open to most everything at this point. Does it involve Kama Sutra again?"

"You wish!"

"Like you don't!"

"I'm only human, you know."

"Not the part I remember. That was all animal. Oh, hell, I'm too tired to tease you. Isn't that just the shits? What's the idea?"

"I have a water revitalization machine coming on board today. I want you to try it."

"Does this involve being naked or anything like that?"

"No!"

"Well, damn. You're no fun."

"It's based on the Caduceus I found in Greece."

"Based on the what?"

"The Caduceus. You know the universal sign of healing."

"I know the Caduceus. I was a paramedic before I finished nursing school. We had a little brass one on our collar. What does that have to do with your machine?"

"My machine is a Caduceus, made out of copper, wound around a ferrite core and energized by direct current."

"Do dee, do do." Cassidy made the sing-song theme music from the Twilight Zone.

"Go on, mock me out. They laughed at Einstein, too."

"It was his hair."

"I could give you the dime tour." Francis asked attempting to bring nostalgia to the situation.

"Okay, but it's more like I have energy for the nickel tour."

When they got in the car and moved into traffic, Francis brought Cassidy up to date on the history of the Caduceus, the King Solomon bowl, the staff of Moses, the use of the staff and serpent as an actual device as opposed to a symbol, and his conviction that the device was a real healing vessel after he found the remnant in Greece. He made a convincing argument as they drove toward her hotel.

"Why don't you stay with me while you're in town?" he asked her as they pulled up to the hotel.

"I'll need my strength. Thanks all the same. You don't think I could resist riding you like a cowboy again?"

"There doesn't need to be anything else." He said in protest.

"Oh, yes, there would be. Desperate dying women want their nooky."

"Don't say that." Francis quickly responded.

"I work Hospice. I know dying people when I see them. It's okay, Francis. I can face it. I help people face death every day. It's got me in its grip. I know it. I know how to face it and I know how to fight it. I'm okay. Really I am."

"What are they going to do for you?"

"I have a treatment plan worked out. Nurses are a pain to help; really, they know everything that should be done. The hard part for me is to be a patient. I've spent most of my life on the other side. It's awkward for me."

"Do you want to drop by the lab?"

"Now?"

"Yes. Why not?"

"You know, it might be a good idea. I've got the jitters about tomorrow anyway. A little something to take my mind off it wouldn't hurt."

Francis pulled back into traffic. "I wanted to ask you something anyway. It's a little bit of an odd question."

"Go on, ask your odd question. Can't be anymore odd than the few days we spent together, hanging from the steps under a church, meeting Theodora, the missing monk and that send-off I got."

"What send-off?"

"Didn't I tell you? Theodora came to call once more."

"What happened?"

"She slammed the door and then turned on the water faucet. I got the hell out of there."

"It's relevant, my question, to Theodora's visit."

"How so?"

"Do you believe in spirits and such?" Francis looked directly at her when he asked the question. His car veered toward a parked car and he jerked it back in the lane.

"Be careful, Francis. You'll end up killing me before I die." They both laughed.

It was the first time they had laughed. The mood in the car lightened. Cassidy continued, "I guess I believe in a spirit or something after life. I have seen a lot of strange things attending to people as they die. I did some research about the end of life and attended a conference about care at the end of life, but no one talks much about the spiritual aspect of dying. Well, that's not exactly true, a lot of people talk about dying as a religious event, but not many people are interested in the remains of the cognitive life once the body has died."

"Do you think people can be healed, spiritually healed?" Francis asked tentatively.

"That's a hard one for me, particularly now. I have been with families as their loved ones hovered near death, and they prayed with sincerity for a healing miracle and it didn't work. I have seen more disappointments at the end of prayers than healings. When at last it is obvious the healing isn't coming, people resign themselves by accepting the will of God."

"It is a hard question, I know, but it relates to the power of the Caduceus and other experiments I have read about healing water. It seems that the water can in some manner anticipate the expectations or resonate somehow with the desire for healing."

"Francis, that's the old argument that faith healers use when they can't heal someone, they blame the person for not believing enough that they are going to be healed. If you look for objective evidence for healing substances, you can see that a healing substance works on the conscious mind or the unconscious mind. The substance itself brings about a change without regard of the belief of the patient. Morphine brings relief of pain because it blocks pain receptors. As a scientist you can see the clinical consequence of a morphine drip. It can be measured."

"Yes, but studies on pain show that pain is an ambiguous element. People report widely differing degrees of pain in similar experiences. Some patients report feeling better when given sugar pills if they believed the pills would bring relief. Some patients heal more quickly if they express belief in the methods used by their doctors and nurses. There is a definite mental or intentional component to healing."

"People who are dying clutch a lot of straws. Is your question whether or not I believe in belief?" Cassidy asked and waited.

Francis' reply was slow and deliberate, "I guess you could put it that way."

"Then, yes, I do believe that people believe and from that belief, events can happen in their life differently than if they did not believe."

"What then of healing? Do you think people have been healed by acts of faith alone?"

"I think it takes more, some catalyst for the healing, whether it is Divine touch, magic potions or chemotherapy, something must intervene at precisely the right moment. Francis, I don't have any evidence for this belief about healing. It is more intuitive or perhaps informed by stories of healing that I've read. In the ancient days and in primitive cultures today, people are healed by methods we do not understand. Voodoo, for instance, can make people die, because of a curse or because they think they will die and they may create a toxic shock syndrome inside themselves, I don't know."

"If I told you the Caduceus would heal you if you believed it would, what would your response be."

"It's the same clap trap as the traveling preacher in a revival tent that does a healing and no one gets better. He will tell them that they would have been healed if they had a stronger faith, more belief. The responsibility is always put on the patient instead of the magic."

"Did you ever hear of the healing stick Moses carried through the desert?"

"You mean the one Charleston Heston laid down and it turned into a snake?"

"Yes, that's the one. The same one he used to push the waters of the sea apart, to touch a stone to make a spring come forth to give his people water, and the one he used to heal serpent bites."

"I only know about the water parting and the snake thing."

"Throughout time there has always been the magic staff that actually became the magic wand. The wand in concert with the mind of the magician does wondrous things."

"Like in Harry Potter?"

"Yes, or Lord of the Rings. The wand or staff has power and has endured across centuries. Many kings used such staffs as signs of power. The Caduceus is a staff of power and the snake or snakes, depending on which model you use, empowers the staff to heal."

"There is the magic crystal thing too, right?" Cassidy asked with sincerity.

"Well, it is depicted as many things. It has gone from being a stone in Egyptian representations to a stone with wings. The winged stone turned stylistically into a Phoenix bird or other symbols of power, such as an angel. Like in the movies, the stick has a glowing stone on top. I think the glowing is a representation like the wings. I think they were meteorites. Meteors are flying stones that glow, or glowed when they fell to the earth and were found. I think that life on earth was seeded by such a stone that fell into the primordial seas and sparked life. These stones were used by the ancients in their healing ceremonies and ancient sacred places, all lined up with the stars. They tried to align the stones with their places of origin to give them increased power."

"Wasn't there quite a stir recently that a meteorite was suspected of showing signs of microbial life?"

"Now and then this idea emerges, that life was seeded by the universe, but until life is found outside our own earth, it remains a speculation."

"Francis, do you believe the Caduceus will heal me?"

"I hope so."

Francis pulled up to a parking lot gatehouse. He showed the guard his badge and signed a visitor form for Cassidy. They parked in a spot near a squat non-descript building. Francis slid his identification card across the reader by the front door and they were admitted to a hallway. He walked toward two security guards seated outside a set of large metal double doors.

Once again he slid his identification card through the reader and opened one of the double doors. Cassidy and Francis entered the darkened room and he flipped on the lights. Cassidy stepped back with a gasp to absorb what greeted her: a vertical seven-foot rod of stone inside two entwining, spiraling tubes of copper.

Francis watched her and began his explanation, "The tubes cross each other six times and at each crossing point they are at 90 degree angles with each other. The rod core is made of ferrite, an iron bearing stone that has natural magnetic properties."

Cassidy followed him as he walked around and continued, "On the sides of the copper tubes, electric wires lead to a line of batteries. A large switch separates the tubes from the electricity source. The tops of the copper tubes have a large opening above which glass beakers of spring water are hung. The copper tubes decrease in diameter as they come to the bottom, much as a snake is fatter at the top of its body than at the tail. The openings at the tail empty into a beaker designed to collect the water. This mark on the floor is for the beaker."

"Who's funding this research, the Science Fiction Channel?" Cassidy managed to say. She had walked toward the imposing structure and reached out her hands to touch it.

"Careful!" Francis called out. "You better not touch it. It may generate electricity."

Chapter 20

"How it works is really quite simple." Francis said as Cassidy studied the Caduceus device. "Pure water is introduced into the spirals as the patient stands close to the device. Direct current is applied to the device and the device and the patient establish a common electrical wave length."

"Simple?" Cassidy said with her eye brows arched.

"It is a matter of internal and external locus of control meeting. The problem with our current view of healing is that healing is an external event brought on by the introduction of a substance, such as an antibiotic. Ancient healing required a partnership between the healer and the healed. It is a kind of resonance that can be enhanced by the use of certain substances or rituals. The release of the reality of daily life is required so the patient enters a state of liminality, a kind of betwixt and between state of belief in the process of healing and in the interior ability to be healed. What is needed to make it work is the catalyst. In this case, that is the Caduceus. Perhaps it is the symbolism of the entwined snakes, or perhaps the electrical energy given off by the falling water in a charged electric field provided by the ferrite core, or perhaps it is the meteorite at the top. It might be the water itself that changes our cell structures as it nourishes our blood and carries the healing throughout our bodies. I don't really know yet."

"You are asking me to suspend my belief in the known effects of medicine and accept the innate ability of the body to heal itself." Cassidy protested.

"You are a nurse. Explain to me why treatments work on some patients and not on others. Explain to me how two people are exposed to the same injury yet one heals and the other dies. We have grown up in a culture of illness that has explained all human ailments as microbial and all healing as an equivalent intervention. Yet we know that all across the world people are being healed in primitive societies with rituals and cures that defy explanation."

"You are talking about the effect of placebos, the so-called placebo effect, right?"

"Perhaps. People getting better when there is no intervention aside from the belief that the substance they took was healing. It must be attributed to some kind of interior ability to bring about the healing. Take the laying on of hands often mentioned in healing ceremonies. We know that each person has a unique electric wave length signature given off by the body as it does the bio/electric work of living. This kind of direct electrical stimulation may signal the body to open a pathway for the internalized healing process."

"I suppose an argument could be made that all healing is an act of faith." Cassidy could see the validity in Francis' description of healing. "As a nurse, however, I have come to put my faith in medical science."

"And what happens when medical science reaches the end of its knowledge and people are confronted with the final reality of their own death?"

"People turn to faith in their last hours because faith is all they have when all else has been taken away."

"So, in the end, people resort to faith. If faith is a choice, then why not make it a choice at the beginning of illness? Why wait until the illness has taken hold so strongly that extraordinary faith is required to bring about a change? We have been seduced by science to think that only science will cure us. Everyone in science felt that acupuncture was a complete sham until it worked. A process that is based on the body's electrical fields cures illness, yet it has no basis in medical science."

Francis watched her face and offered his next argument. "Cassidy, I am a scientist, but I believe that science and faith do interact. The Caduceus was an instrument of science, quite the advancement for the times in which it was conceived, but it had to work in concert with the patient's faith. Perhaps that is why it fell out of favor, because people were seduced by advances in medical science to a point that they could no longer believe in the unseen forces of nature."

Cassidy once again moved closer to the Caduceus. "Explain to me what I am looking at. It looks like something from a bad science fiction film."

"Of course. That is a ferrite core. Ferrite is essentially iron ore. The core was made for me by special order from a quarry. The diameter is seven inches. I used the number seven for several reasons. It is seven feet tall. The copper tubes cross at six points into a cohesive whole, six plus the whole makes seven. The top diameter of the tubes is larger than the bottoms. The tubes reproduce the basic spiral structures of DNA and mimic the body shape of a snake. This is a simple hydrological process known to increase the speed of the falling water by constricting the movement into ever narrow passageways."

Francis moved around the Caduceus, "The electrical charge is enhanced by the capacity of falling water to make static electricity, much the way a shower invigorates the environment as the water falls over the body. I selected direct current because the flow of magnetic energy is in a single direction. I am using a series of interconnected direct current batteries to amplify the charge."

Cassidy followed him as he continued, "The water I use is natural spring water, the same water used in the White House and the Senate, so I am confident of its purity. Natural spring water has a greater spiral potentiality than tap water or reservoir water. As the water falls through the electrified field and enters a forced spiral it gains internalized spirals at the molecular level. I am convinced this, in interaction with the patient's own energy field, produces the potential for healing."

"So, this is the healing machine?"

"Well, not exactly, it has to work in concert with the patient. It does not heal. It sets the internal conditions or opens a healing gate, to be more accurate. Some devices may make the body open the healing mechanisms more effectively than others. I am convinced the Caduceus device the ancients used did this. I made this model based on a life-time study of the artistic renditions of the Caduceus as well as on the brass Caduceus I found in Greece."

"Well, turn the sucker on and give me a drink." Cassidy said extending her hands.

"It's not that simple. You need to prepare yourself."

"Oh, I get it. This is where the naked dancing takes place." She gave him a sardonic smile.

"No! Well, not right now anyway." He gave the tease back to her. "You need to put your mind in a place of openness about the possibility, actually a bit stronger than that, you need assurance that this will work for you. Light-hearted tolerance of the idea is not the same as whole scale acceptance. You need to get to that place that is between one reality and the other. The place between doubt and faith opens your mind. That is what is meant by liminality. People achieve liminality by using rituals to prepare themselves to enter slightly altered states, such as a light hypnosis."

"I find myself between life and death, is that liminal enough for you?"

"Place yourself in the situation as a peasant that has traveled hundreds of miles in a desperate trek to a healer's location at a temple that has a history of healing people. You are surrounded by first-hand accounts of healing at this location by this device and the holy man who uses it. You have as much cultural belief in this device as modern patients do in penicillin. You approach the device and are asked to give a prayer for healing, thus opening your mind and body for healing. You are unaware of electricity in your daily life in a village. You approach the device and touch it. You feel the electricity in your hand. Then it surges through your body and you interpret the electrical sensation as a confirmation of the healing taking place. You open the healing place within you by this belief confirmed in sensory stimulations moving through out your body."

Francis paused. Cassidy remained very quiet, listening. He continued, "The device senses and adjusts its electric field to your own unique wave length signature. You and the device are connected for a moment as the healing energy, either produced by your belief in it or by some process of bio-electrical energy we do not understand. Your cells alter. Perhaps they only alter slightly, enough to prevent the reproduction of invading cells or strengthen the cells walls to prevent the invading germs and viruses from entering them. By whatever means it happens, it happens. You begin to feel better almost instantly. The invading cells, deprived of nurturance, die. You return to your village and tell the story of your healing and the next person approaches the Caduceus with cultural confidence and it works for them, as it did for you."

"Does your grant fund the making of healing water?"

"That, I cannot tell you. Let me say that they are interested in helping our troops in the field stay healthy."

Cassidy walked around the device. She had placed her arms around herself, her hands in her arm pits. She seemed to be talking to herself. After several turns around the device she stood suddenly in front of it. She bowed her head for a moment.

"I'm ready." She said.

Chapter 21

"Miss Martin. Cassidy Martin?" A young nurse stuck her head out behind a door inside Sloan-Kettering's clinic for breast cancer. Cassidy rose and put her magazine on the seat. She had been waiting for nearly thirty minutes past her appointment time. The nurse spoke first, "I'm sorry you had to wait. It's been a very busy day."

Cassidy started to say something to reduce the stress she was sure the young nurse was feeling. She remembered times when she had been the nurse dealing with people waiting for appointments long delayed by others' emergencies. Now, however, instead of making light of the situation, she gave the young nurse a steely-eyed stare. The nurse walked silently ahead leading Cassidy to an examination room.

"The doctor will be right with you." The young nurse pushed a plastic paddle outside the door to show the room was occupied and closed the door. The examination table seemed coldly foreign to Cassidy. She sat instead on a stool with wheels. She rolled herself to the window and lifting the mini-blinds looked outside at the world below. Beneath her on the lawn a young girl played with a styrofoam cup. She was filling it with blades of grass then pouring them out into little piles.

Several more moments passed before a knock came on the door and a middle-aged man presented himself as Doctor Marlow. He looked at her on the stool and motioned for her to take a seat on the table, "I have had a chance to look at your films sent ahead by Doctor Dean."

Cassidy made no reply. She found herself feeling angry.

Dr. Marlow spoke again, "I want to do a set of my own for comparison."

Cassidy remained quiet.

"Is that all right with you Miss, or is that Mrs. Martin?"

"I don't see what difference that makes!" she quipped back.

"You are right, Cassidy. May I call you Cassidy?" The doctor asked tentatively.

"I sat out there for thirty minutes waiting on you." She finally managed.

"Yes. I know. We had a very difficult case and it took a little longer than – "

"A little longer? Do you know what it is like, sitting out there?"

"I can imagine it is stressful. It is stressful just being here, isn't it?"

"What would you know about it?" She stared at him.

The doctor took on a fundamental joining posture, giving back to Cassidy her words in an attempt to sooth her, "I hear you saying it is stressful to be here."

"Look. Don't play games with me. I'm a nurse. I know the routine."

"All right, I see. I am aware you are a nurse. It seems to me that you are feeling quite angry right now. Would you like me to step out for a moment?"

"What? And waste another thirty minutes? I don't think so. Could we get to the point here, Poindexter, or whatever your name is?"

"Marlow. It is Doctor Marlow. Are you on any current medications?"

"Noooo! I just thought a diet coke and an enema would fix me."

"I see. Okay, then. Let's start again. Any medications?"

"This is my cheerful self, okay? I'm not loopy on drugs if that's the question."

"That's not my question. You know, Cassidy, being here and having cancer produces a lot of anger. It's perfectly normal for you to be feeling angry."

"Let's clear something up here, doctor. I'm not normal, nor did I ever intend to have a life that was normal. If I were angry, you would know very damn well and certain that I was angry." Now shouting at him she declared, "I am not angry!"

"About those films then, since, as you say, you are not angry. I want to take the films Doctor Dean sent along and do some comparison x-rays to see how the tumor's progressing."

The doctor kept his pen on the paper attached to a clip board. The door pushed open as the young nurse tapped on the door, "Doctor Marlow, do you have a moment?" she asked.

Cassidy jumped to her feet, "Goddamn it, get out! I spent a fucking hour in your waiting room and I just now got to see Dork Duffer here and I'm not waiting another thirty minutes while you take him down the hall for a blow job."

Both the nurse and Doctor Marlow stared at her. Cassidy found herself standing with both fists raised above her head. The realization that she had lost her temper came over her suddenly. Tears welled up in her eyes and she fled out the door.

Cassidy pushed her way through the waiting room and back into the hallway where she found a restroom. She went into a stall, locked the door and sat down sobbing. When she had blown her nose several times and felt like she could breathe again, she found her cell phone in her purse and called Francis.

"Allenton here," his voice was calm.

"Francis? This is Cassidy. I can't believe what I just did. I just bit the head off a perfectly nice doctor and his nurse over here."

"Cassidy, calm down, you're just anxious. It is perfectly normal to be anxious about all this."

"No, no, listen to me! I just roared at the people who are trying to help me. I know stress as a consequence of having cancer and I know what medications I am on will do to you and this is not anything like that. This is full tilt, balls to the wall, homicidal anger. I've never felt like this before. Francis, what the hell was in that water you gave me?"

"Cassidy, absolutely nothing is in that water. It's spring water from Arkansas. It has been bottled and delivered to my lab for experimentation. There isn't anything in that water to make you hostile."

"Are you sure?" Cassidy asked, finding it hard to believe her anger was brought on by her own reaction to pain medication or stress. "Francis, answer this for me, the water from the Caduceus, have you tested it on anyone?"

"Well, no. We just hooked it up the day you got here."

"Are you telling me that I'm your only goddamned guinea pig?"

"No! I wouldn't do that to you. Calm down. I am certain there is a perfectly rational explanation for what just happened to you. Do you need me to come over there?"

Cassidy thought about his request. She felt calmer now. She wondered if it was because she'd talked to him or was it some kind of calm that comes after you lose your temper and blow up. She felt drained. "No. I'm better now. I'm going to go back in there and try to make it right. I'll call you when I'm done here. Maybe we can have dinner later. I'm calm now."

"You're sure?"

"Yes, well, I'm pretty sure. It just came over me like a huge wave of anger. I was acting like a mad woman in there."

"Please, Cassidy, call me if you need me. I'll come over there immediately."

"Thanks, bye. I'll call you later." Cassidy unlocked the door and went over to the sink. She threw some water on her face, and then looked in the mirror. Her reflection was not comforting, but she fixed her make-up, and walked back to the reception area. She tapped on the window. The woman behind the window slid it open just a fraction of an inch.

"I'm back. Don't worry, honey, I don't bite." Cassidy said to her. "I want to see the doctor again."

A different nurse came out to get her. Neither of them said anything. After Cassidy apologized to Doctor Marlow, he did an exam and she went down the hallway to an x-ray area. The process went smoothly, but Cassidy found herself once again becoming agitated. This time it seemed more gradual, but not as intense. She asked for a glass of water and sat in the exam room trying to calm down. She was able to steady her breathing and feel less anxious.

Doctor Marlow came back into the room with the new films. He pushed them into receptacles and turned on the lights. Outlined pictures of her right breast were illuminated. On the left were the films sent by Doctor Dean. A white circle outlined an obvious tumor. The films on the right were clear.

"I don't understand, Miss Martin. Are these the films you brought with you?" He pointed to the films on the left.

"Yes. They are marked with my name and signed by Doctor Dean."

"Come a little closer, will you. You're a nurse and I want your opinion of these films on the right. What do you see?"

Cassidy rose from her seat on the exam table and approached the films. She leaned close to them. She studied both those on the right and the ones Marianna had sent with her. Doctor Marlow took down the first film and inserted it above the second film. He walked to the window and held them up to the sunlight side by side and then overlapping. He returned them both to the illuminated viewing area and lowering his head looked over his glasses at Cassidy.

"Well?" he said. "What's your opinion?"

"Your x-ray machine is obviously defective." She said grinning at him.

He responded with a smile, "I don't think so. When were you diagnosed?"

"Thirty-three days ago."

"Excuse me a moment." Doctor Marlow stepped out of the room. He returned a few minutes later with a portable sonogram machine and a technician. "Let's have a better look, shall we?"

Cassidy lay on the exam table. Doctor Marlow applied jell and touched the broad head of the sonogram wand to the area of her right breast where the biopsy had sampled a tumor. He turned the screen toward Cassidy.

"Have you undergone any treatment thus far?"

"No."

"Nothing?"

"No chemotherapy or radiation?" he asked incredulously.

"No."

"Any change in diet, exercise, anything?"

"Just spring water!"

"Well, you know how to read this as well as I. There is nothing here." He turned off the sonogram and had the technician take the cart out of the room. Doctor Marlow took a seat. Cassidy watched him. He removed his glasses and put them in his pocket. He was a nice-looking man, a bit disheveled, but pleasant to look at. He had wavy hair that had mostly gone white. He crossed his legs revealing brightly colored socks. He sat silently for a moment. Cassidy sat quietly.

Suddenly he got up and walked over to the window. For what seemed several minutes he stood looking out into the bright afternoon. Then he turned and fixed his eyes on hers. His eyes moved back and forth in a searching manner, hoping to see something deep within Cassidy's eyes to reveal the answer to a question he needed to ask.

"Are you a religious person, Cassidy?"

"Not terribly."

"No revivals or healing crusades on your schedule last month?"

"No, sir. God and I aren't exactly on speaking terms."

"Oh, really. Anything odd happen to you recently?"

"Like what?"

"I don't know, little green men in flying saucers. That kind of thing?"

"I have a boyfriend, sort of." Cassidy decided to hide the strange events that occurred when she stood in front of Francis' Caduceus. She noticed that Doctor Marlow had a medical pin in his lapel. The universal medical symbol of the Caduceus was attached to his lab coat.

"We have a research program going on here, Cassidy. I wonder if you would indulge me and give a blood sample?"

"What kind of research?"

"We call it the spontaneous remission program."

"You think I am in remission?"

"Cassidy, what I think is, I think you are healed, without cause or explanation. However, since we're all a bunch of skeptics around here about spontaneous healing, I will put it down in the chart as remission."

"Okay, but about the blood sample, can you make it quick. I really need to get out of here."

As a nurse Cassidy respected the need for research, but she thought she could feel another wave of anger building. She was mystified and frustrated. Right now she wanted to be feeling elated, ready to celebrate, but this searing anger left no room for joy. By the time the technician came to the room and took the sample from her arm Cassidy was pacing the room.

"Goddamn time you showed up. If you hurt me when you poke me with that, I'm going to give it to you rectally."

It was the smoothest blood draw of the technician's career.

Chapter 22

Cassidy's exit and walk through the reception area was a blur to her. She took the stairs down the three flights to the street level. She didn't trust herself in an elevator with other people. She wondered if she was losing her mind. Her tumbling thoughts, the roller coaster of feelings, her impulses were flowing. She muttered under her breath mocking people as they passed her. A delivery man bumped her and she gave him the finger. She kept walking and then, once again, she found shelter in the first restroom she could find. She found herself sitting on the stool and pushing the sides of the stall as hard as she could with her hands. She waited, but no tears came. Pulling out her cell phone, she hit the call button twice.

"Allenton."

"Francis, you pecker-headed son of a bitch, what have you done to me?"

"Cassidy! My God, where are you? Are you at the clinic?"

"I don't know who the hell I am, let alone where."

"Stay where you are, I'll come get you."

"You weren't listening, were you? I do not know where I am."

"What did they say? Is it worse then you thought? None of this makes sense."

"No. Hell, they say I'm healed. It's your fucking water. It took away the cancer and turned me into Hitler."

"Healed? What are you saying? What do you mean, healed?"

"Healed. Just like on Sunday morning television, praise the Lord and pass the collection plate." She was nearly incoherent now. She was raging and laughing at the same time. She dropped her phone on the floor and continued yelling, "What the hell did you do to me?"

Francis heard a clunk, but at least he could hear her sobbing. He said her name several times and waited hoping she'd speak into the phone again.

When she did, her voice was soft and vacant of emotion. "Come and get me, Francis. I don't feel very well. Come and get me."

"I'll come right away. Can you find an address?"

"It's a big building not far from the Clinic."

"Can you go outside?"

"I'm trying to stay away from people, but maybe I can. Hold on a moment." Francis waited without speaking.

Cassidy walked out of the bathroom. "Francis, I'm at the front doors now. I'm pretty sure that the Clinic is about a block away on my left and across the street is a Starbucks."

"Got it. I can find you. I should be able to get to you in twenty minutes. Thank God it's not rush hour. Don't leave."

"Come and get me, Francis. I don't feel very good at all."

Thirty minutes later Francis saw Cassidy sitting on a park bench several blocks down from the Clinic. He double parked and ran toward her. She was engaged in a yelling match with a young man. She was slurring cuss words and his face was red with rage. Stepping between them, Francis just missed a left-hand blow from Cassidy before he led her quickly to the car.

"Leave me alone. I'm waiting for my boyfriend, leave me alone." Cassidy said under her breath. She looked as if she were in shock. Francis tucked her in the back seat with a blanket around her. She offered no resistance. He pushed the kid locks for the back doors and drove.

When he got to his apartment, he led her up the stairs and helped her stretch out on his bed. He pulled out his ringing cell phone "Allenton here."

"Francis, my boy, this is Alford Purlough. I was hoping to meet with you today. Did I have our appointment wrong? I thought it was for 4 p.m. today."

"I'm so sorry, Mister Purlough. It's my girlfriend. She has taken ill."

"The same lady that visited the lab yesterday?" Purlough asked.

"Yes, sir. How did you know?"

"We always have our guest check in, remember? You signed her in. Nothing serious I hope?"

"It could be. She's here at Sloan-Kettering for treatment."

"Oh, dear, that is serious. Perhaps we can meet tomorrow then?"

"That would be so kind of you, sir. Thank you."

"Not at all. I was just wondering about your preliminary results."

"The agitation formula is nearly worked out. We had some interesting results with the Rhesus monkey yesterday. I think it will be ready to go on schedule. As soon as Mark gets here we can move along at a much faster pace."

"I have some disappointing news about your friend. It seems Mark got into some trouble with the authorities in the past. I'm certain his security clearance will be denied."

"Denied? How bad can it be?"

"Bad enough. I have a man I'm sending over in the next few days to assist you."

"What man?"

"A man that has worked for us before. He will be invaluable to you. Doctor Yan Lin. Have you heard of him?"

"Chinese, isn't he. I think I have read some of his articles." A crash in the bedroom told Francis that Cassidy was up. "I really have to go now, sir. I'll make that appointment with you tomorrow, same time."

"Until tomorrow then."

Francis found Cassidy sitting up in bed.

"I feel like shit!"

"You look like shit." Francis smiled at her.

"That's my guy, always full of flattery. That and a beer will get you laid."

"How are you feeling?"

"Come see for yourself." Cassidy rocked provocatively for a moment and then holding her head she fell back onto the bed. "What a headache I have."

"You've been busy."

"Doing what?"

"Pissing off the Pope, it seems."

"I don't remember. Hey, did I get into a fight with a man on the street?"

"You remember all right."

"No! Really?"

"So it seems. What's all this about being healed?"

"Nothing on the x-ray. I'm healed, the good doctor said. I gave them a blood sample and got the hell out of there before I made a fool out of myself again."

"Healed completely?"

"I know what you're thinking."

"What did you tell them?"

"Nothing."

"Didn't they ask?"

"Seems they get a lot of that around there. So much so they have a special research project."

"I'd love to talk to them over there."

"And what? Tell them about your magic machine?"

"You know I can't tell anyone, and for that matter, neither can you."

"Why not? What if it healed me? You can't keep something like that for yourself."

"I'm not. There would have to be trials and double-blind studies and all that before we could let it get out. You know the way it goes with new discoveries. Besides, the lab is secret. I shouldn't have even brought you in there. I was just so excited to show you around."

"Listen, Francis, what if it does work?"

"Then we have an obligation to return it to the world."

"Will they let you?"

"It's the World Health Organization, of course, they will."

Chapter 23

Cassidy had a fitful night. She awoke to find Francis already at work. He had left her a sweet note. She decided to call Marianna Dean.

"Is Dean there?" she asked the receptionist.

"Dean here."

"It's me."

"What did they say?"

"I'm already dead. I'm calling you from heaven. I have bad news. Your first husband is here. I guess that pretty much means you're going to hell."

"If he is in heaven, you better be damn sure I will want a reservation in hell. Now, tell me what they said. They faxed me a set of blood results I don't understand at all. Why did they send them to me? Aren't you there?"

"They discharged me. Actually, they never admitted me."

"What? Those guys promised me they would get you in."

"No need. I'm clear."

"Clear?"

"As a glass of water." Cassidy said.

"I don't get it. What are you saying?"

"I no longer have a date with destiny, well, not a quick date anyway."

"You know, Cassidy, I love you and all, but quit jerking me around."

"I'm not."

"Well, how? Why? What did they do?"

"Absolutely nothing. I got in, saw the doctor, nearly took his balls off by the way, and he did a set of films and nothing was there."

"I don't get it. You saw your films here. I'm confident there was a mass and the biopsy showed cancer."

"Where did you get that license anyway?"

"Stop it. Stop it right now. If you are jerking me around I'm going to kick your skinny little ass."

"Listen to me. I'm serious. There was nothing on the film."

"Your blood scores they sent me are weird. You have an extraordinary amount of manganese."

"What the hell is that?"

"It's a mineral. Have you been doing supplements from that health store again?"

"No. Manganese?"

"Like I said, manganese. You know, as in manganese madness."

"What's that you said? Say it again."

"Manganese madness. It comes from too much manganese in your blood stream."

"What are the effects?"

"Hell, there is only one direct effect. You end up trying to kill everyone you come into contact with. How are you feeling now?"

"Very tired and very anxious."

"Are you coming home right away?"

"No. There is something I have to do here first."

"When you get here we'll do another blood test. At any rate, call me, again soon, Cass, and let me know for sure when you're coming home. Girl, you better not be just pushing my buttons here."

"I'll call you when I have my tickets home. Promise. Pick me up?"

"Of course."

Cassidy called Sloan-Kettering.

"Is Doctor Marlow there? Yes. This is Cassidy Martin. Yes. I'll hold."

"Cassidy?"

"Yes. I was wondering if you got the results back from yesterday's blood."

"Yes. We faxed them to your doctor. Are you still in town?"

"Yes."

"I would like to have you come back in. There is something in the blood that puzzles me."

"The manganese level?"

"You've talked to Doctor Dean already?"

"Yes. Is there anything else?"

"I looked at the blood under the microscope this morning. It's most strange."

"How so?"

"You have had changes in your blood's cell structure. The cytoskeletal microfilaments have altered. The cell adhesion is also altered. The cancer cells are isolated and cannot move or reproduce. They are quickly dying of starvation, for lack of a better word."

"That's a good thing, right?"

"It is the best thing that could happen. The cancer cells have lost their motility, their capability to spontaneously move. They also appear to have lost their ability to adhere to other cells so no mass can form. In addition to this, the other cells are containing them so they cannot move or migrate to any other location. The healthy cells seem to have increased their ability to withstand invasion from the cancer cells, perhaps because the cancer cells cannot produce the enzymes to break down their barriers. I just can't tell right now. We have been attempting to create this sequence in the lab. This is most exciting. You must come back in right away."

Chapter 24

Across town Francis had arrived at his lab. Immediately he saw that things had been moved from their original positions. A man, whom Francis presumed to be Doctor Yan Lin, was giving instructions to some men who were rearranging the lab table.

Francis moved toward him with a degree of authority. Francis was aware that two scientists in the same lab often resulted in a jousting match for dominance.

"Doctor Lin. It's a pleasure to have you join my project."

Doctor Lin gave him a non-responsive yet polite acknowledgment.

"Doctor Allenton. Good morning. I have taken the liberty of making a few changes in the flow of the equipment. I hope you approve."

"Things were working quite well as they were, thank you. Dr. Lin, I have lost track of you in the literature for the last several years. You defected from China, as I recall, in order to expand your work on enzymes."

"That is correct." Lin returned to his task of moving lab equipment.

"Excuse me, Lin, is that absolutely necessary?" Francis asked. He touched Lin's shoulder to get his attention. Lin spun around and his earlier smile was gone.

"We have a deadline, Doctor. I am used to meeting my deadlines. The group that is funding this research has asked me to assure that regular progress is made."

"I am the principal investigator." Francis reasserted his position.

"Ah, yes. How important titles are to Westerners. Most assuredly you are the principal investigator. My role, while it lacks the formality of a title, is equally important. This is a results-oriented study with a timeline. I will not direct the line of inquiry, but I will be reporting on a daily basis any breakthroughs or discoveries that we make. I can assure you that Mister Purlough has approved my placement in the lab, and I act with complete authority from the Cartel."

"Cartel?"

"Did I say Cartel. My English has failed me again. I meant to say Committee. May I ask how the mineralization study is going?"

"The study has shown results in the Rhesus. His aggression was fairly vigorous soon after administration of the formulated water. We are removing the aggressive element by progressive sieve filter techniques. The mineral we used shows promise in preventing the release of self-calming agents, such as dopamine, while at the same time it releases excitatory neurotransmitters."

"The mineralized water reduces dopamine and increases adrenalin?" Lin asked.

"Is there any evidence that the water memory hypothesis is valid?"

"I was not aware that such an obscure study would have caught your attention."

"We do read in China, Doctor Allenton."

"There seems to be no validity to the notion of water memory at this point."

"How many minerals and agents have you reviewed?"

"We just got started last week. So far we are reviewing the minerals found naturally in spring water. We have a supply brought in each day."

"Very good. Your reputation is not unfounded." Lin walked toward the Caduceus.

"And I suppose this is the famous Caduceus machine you proposed? I am surprised they allowed you to indulge your fantasies. At the most, all you can expect is highly charged water molecules."

"The thesis has merit. There are a number of studies that show – "

"Piffle paffle!" Lin interrupted. "Those studies were conducted by morons. Surely you don't think a hydrologist from turn-of-the-century Germany would have discovered the Fountain of Youth."

"It was Austria."

"What?"

"The man was from Austria."

"Wherever! Nothing of substance has ever come from the Europeans. A bunch of druids dressed up in robes sacrificing goats never discovered anything of substance. The cradle of civilization and the discovery of medicine are clearly Chinese in origin."

"Yes, of course. Just look at your country now. China has the largest class of workers unfed and abused, forbidden to have more than one child, and smashed like bugs when they stand up for basic human rights. That's the stuff that progress is made of."

"Let's not quibble, shall we, Doctor Allenton. I no longer work under the People's flag. I have changed my loyalties."

"Yes. Let's not quibble."

Across the lab the telephone rang. Lin looked at Francis. "Well, Doctor Allenton, it is your lab. Perhaps you should answer the phone."

Francis walked away from Lin moving his lips in mock imitation of what Lin had jut said. He picked up the phone.

"Allenton here."

"Francis, it's Cassidy."

"This isn't the best time."

"You are going to want to know this."

"Things coming out of the mirror at you again?"

"Shut up and listen." Cassidy made her voice stern.

"Okay. Make it quick, will you. I've got some unwanted help in the lab today. Cassidy, I'm sorry, I don't mean to be short with you. Are you feeling okay, any better?"

"I haven't taken off anyone's head yet today, but I have some lab results on that blood sample."

"And?"

"And they show that my cells have turned into little super women cells. Somehow the cytoskeletal structures have hardened and the cancer cells are immobile. They aren't going anywhere, so they can't eat or reproduce and they are dying off like ants under a tennis shoe."

"Wow, that is amazing. I would like to take a look at those results. That's great. Really it is. Does this mean the cowboy gets another ride?"

"Honestly, is that all you think about?"

"Honestly? No. I think of other things. How are your mood changes today?"

"I'm calm. Nearly too calm. Weird like I was drug through a wringer. But that's something else I wanted to tell you. The blood sample came back with excessive amounts of manganese."

"Manganese?"

"That's what they said. Doctor Dean said it would make me bite the head off a snake and spit it at the devil."

"She's right. Where in the heck did you get manganese?"

"Well, I thought maybe the Caduceus might have done it somehow."

"While you were in the lab here, did you drink anything else or touch anything at all?"

"Nothing."

"You are certain?"

Francis noticed that Doctor Lin had walked slowly closer and closer to him as he was on the phone. Lin was pretending to do idle work on the lab table, but Francis could tell he was tuned in."

"Well, Doctor, it's been nice talking to you. I will let you know if we have any openings in the future."

"What on earth are you talking about, Francis?" Cassidy asked.

"Perhaps we can visit about this later." Francis hoped Cassidy would know the inflection at the end of his sentence meant that he could not talk openly.

"When will I see you?"

"Tonight? I realize you're in town for just a short time, but, no, thank you just the same. I'll be having dinner with my lady friend around seven."

"Okay. Around seven then."

Francis hung up the phone. He didn't understand how Cassidy could have been exposed to manganese. It was one of the elements he had been testing in the experiments on aggression, but it was a highly controlled substance. Lin approached him at his desk.

"A potential partner on the phone?"

"Yeah. I thought Mark was going to join me and when he couldn't, I made a few calls leaving messages for former colleagues and contacts. I didn't know until yesterday that you would be joining the team."

"Did I hear you say manganese?" Lin asked.

"Did I?"

"I thought so."

"No. I don't think so, perhaps your English failed you again."

Francis busied himself with the experiments on the Rhesus monkey. The animal handlers had reported the monkey had a difficult night following the infusion of manganese into his water. The manganese was being reduced by small amounts until the behavior was documented as returned to normal. Francis was attempting to find the level at which it could be in the water and not bring about a behavioral change.

Lin had gone over to the Caduceus and was standing in front of the device with his hands on his hips. He turned to Francis and asked. "May I have a demonstration?"

"It's not really ready yet, Doctor Lin." Francis lied. "I have a few things to work out."

"How much did this monstrosity cost the project?"

"Fifty-seven thousand and change."

"I suppose they are willing to let you have your fantasies as long as you deliver the research results."

"You mentioned a cartel earlier."

"Did I?"

"Do I remember your area of expertise as psychological warfare?"

"No. I'm not interested in warfare. My interest, like you, is the enhancement of water to bring about desired behavioral, life-saving or health-preserving changes."

"Your writing ceased after you left China. The last thing I remember reading was your study about the manipulation of enzymes to produce behavior changes. Weren't you zeroing in on the specific consequences of certain enzymes on aggression?"

"Yes. That is exactly the line of inquiry I was pursuing. However, like yourself, I have joined the organization to determine if any naturally occurring enzyme that might alter behavior can be removed while other enzymes might be added to water to enhance basic healing properties or aid in resistance to infection in the event of a wound or an exposure to toxic substances."

Lin turned back to the Caduceus, "I was excited to learn that you would be leading the investigation as I have followed your work on revitalization of water. In order for the water to be manipulated, we need the water molecules to be as pristine and receptive as possible. Have you been able to revitalize water from common sources?"

"You mean tap water or reservoir water?"

"Yes. The supply of raw water, from springs or other sources, such as Glacier melt water, is very limited. Eventually very few people on earth will have water supplies from the ancient sources trapped below the earth. Many of these sources of water are from ancient deposits and have remained unchanged for thousands of years. On the main, however, most people in the future will drink water that has been recycled or captured in reservoirs."

"No. I haven't been able to revitalize tap water and other standard sources to any kind of verifiable primitive state."

"So you obviously follow the idea that inherent structures in the water need to be reintroduced, such as spirals? Yes, I can tell from your Caduceus that you intend to spiral the water and add an electric charge. Mister Purlough has informed me that you may have had some interesting results when using spring water."

"I have not had any results of promise. I have discovered nothing that could be verified."

"Yet you persist with this machine." Lin observed.

"It's growing late, Doctor Lin. I propose we take up this topic tomorrow."

"Yes. I'm certain your date with your girlfriend is more important than our discussion at present." He walked through and door and turned to add, "I wish you a pleasant evening."

Francis walked out and locked the door to the lab that contained the Caduceus. He felt an intense dislike of Lin growing. He had not counted on Purlough bringing an outsider into his research project. The mention of a cartel had left Francis very unsettled.

Arriving at his apartment, Francis unlocked the door and threw in a bouquet of roses. When they weren't thrown out the door from within, he presumed Cassidy had remained calm most of the day. He put his head in the door and looked around. Cassidy was sitting at the computer.

"I logged on using my account and was doing some research. I hope you don't mind." Cassidy shut down the computer and came into the kitchen. She noticed the flowers on the floor. "You have flowers on your floor."

"They are for you. I guess we have a celebration of sorts on for tonight. I have a new lab partner and you are no longer psychotic."

"Where is Mark?" Cassidy asked.

"He couldn't get security clearance."

"The World Health Organization has security?"

"Yes, I don't know, terrorist worries or whatever."

"I have been on the internet most of the day."

"Searching Kama Sutra positions again?"

"No. Trying to find Alford Purlough."

"Why in the world?"

"There is no such person in the World Health Organization." Cassidy said.

"It's not exactly the WHO. It's a sub-branch of theirs, the CAC."

"He's not there either."

"Well, I doubt that they would have every employee on the web site."

"Who are you working for, Francis?"

"I told you. The World Health Organization. We are in their building, for God's sake."

"Anybody can rent space in a building. Who have you met there from the W.H.O.?"

"Well, there is me, the lab helpers, and Doctor Lin. He's the guy that came on today."

"Francis, I am not trying to scare you or anything, but I don't think you are working for the World Health Organization, or if you are, you are in a division that is unofficial."

"Don't be ridiculous. Are you still feeling all right?" Francis began to wonder if Cassidy was suffering from the kind of paranoia that comes with exposure to manganese.

"You know what?"

"What?"

"I'm taking you to dinner and on the way I'm going to stop at the lab. I have a set of information about the W.H.O. that was provided to me before I even came here. Then we will go upstairs and I'll show you all the other offices."

"Anybody can rent an office." Cassidy replied.

"You'll see. Are you ready to go?"

"Give me just a second and I'll be ready."

Francis and Cassidy drove to the lab. The gate was open and no guard stood nearby. The building was dark. Francis used his card to enter the building and stared at the double doors down the hallway ahead. The red light was off on the reader for the identification cards. He walked forward and pulled on the left door handle. The door swung open. Cassidy followed close behind him. Reaching over to his left, he flipped on the lights. A completely empty room lay in front of them. The lab, the materials, the monkeys, and the Caduceus were gone.

Chapter 25

Staring at the empty room, Francis slowly walked toward the area that once had housed the Caduceus. Then he turned and looked at Cassidy. He finally took a breath, "So, tell me, Cassidy, did you by any chance find Purlough on the internet?"

"There was only one reference which was in a news article about the purchase of some water rights in Colorado and Arkansas."

"What did it say?"

"Something about water rights being obtained by an undisclosed water conglomerate. Purlough was quoted briefly."

"Do you remember what he said?" Francis asked her.

"No. Not really. It was something about the future of water in America, some reference to the scarcity of water in the future becoming like oil is now."

"As scarce as oil?"

"In the future, he said. Something about the wealth of nations will be determined by water more so than the wealth of nations is now defined by oil reserves."

Francis paced in a tight circle. "I don't know what to think, Cassidy. I have so much information that has crossed my path since I came to New York. In some ways it's like the Caduceus was at one time, a concept that lay in front of me, but the larger picture and its meaning just didn't form a cohesive pattern. Wait, Lin said something about a cartel. He sloughed it off as a mistake, but I wonder?"

"A water cartel? To what purpose? Isn't there plenty of water now?" Cassidy asked.

Francis picked up the telephone receiver from its cradle on the floor. To his surprise there was a dial tone. He punched in Mark's number in Missouri.

"Yo!" Mark answered.

"Mark, it's Francis. Mark? Are you there?"

"Yes, Francis, what is it?"

"Did you receive anything back on your security clearance?"

"You're kidding me, right?"

"No. Why?"

"After that letter you sent me, it was obvious that you didn't think I was up to the job."

"I sent you a letter?"

"Didn't you?"

"What did it say?"

"What is this, Francis?"

"What did the letter say?"

"It said that you felt the scope and depth of the project would require a different level of scholarship than I possessed. Thank you very much, by the way, I am quite confident I could have made a contribution. You know I resigned based on your assurance that I would be on this project. I had to take hat in hand and go back to Palmetto, and God, I hate sucking up to him. Now they have me teaching intro level classes and I'm on six committees. The next stop for me was Paris. Girard called out of the blue and offered us both positions with the European Space Agency. He is on a project looking into ancient water from space. He called when he heard the lab here had closed."

"Mark, I never sent you a letter."

"Francis, I have it right here. No, wait, I got so pissed off I tore it up and pitched it. Francis, listen to me, it was on letterhead, World Health Organization, just like the notice that came to you in the lab."

"Oh, Mark, what's happened to the lab?"

"They took it down. They are going in a new direction. The only reason that lab was running was your reputation. They don't give a shit about water down here, you know that. What's happened to you?"

"They let me build the Caduceus. God, it was beautiful and it works."

"I would pay good money to see that. I don't get it. If you didn't send me a letter, who did?"

"Well, I have an idea about that, but I am going to need your help."

"So, I was too stupid to help you last month and now you need me."

"Mark, come on, you're the smartest guy I know."

"Next to you?"

"No. Really, I always have had and still have great admiration for you. I'm sorry about the letter. You have to believe me. I did not send you a letter. They told me you couldn't get the security clearance and they had me under a secrecy agreement so I couldn't talk to anyone about the research."

"What was the research about? Can you tell me now? What's happened?"

"I was looking into aggression-producing enzymes. Yan Lin was here."

"Lin? Doctor Yan Lin?"

"Yeah."

"Francis, I saw him last year at the International Water Conference."

"I don't think you said anything when you got back."

"Perhaps not, I saw him at a reception put on by one of the major cola companies. He told me he was working for the G8 and some kind of a water cartel. Now you know how he comes across, like God picked him to save the world."

"I noticed. Did he say anything else about the cartel?"

"No. When I pressed him on it, he dismissed me. Arrogant son of a bitch, isn't he? He did say something about the world population explosion and diminished water production capacity. Isn't he the enzyme guy?"

"Yeah, he was on enzymes and behavior changes." Francis began to see something in a pattern. "Hold on, hold on. Did he make a presentation at that conference?"

"I don't know. If he did, I didn't go to it." Mark searched his memory. "I've got the program in the file. No, hold on, I think I have that conference stuff in one of my boxes right here. I've had to pack up some of my things to take them home."

Francis could hear him rummaging through boxes, papers rattled.

"Yeah, here you go. Francis, here it is. 'Enzyme alterations of moods in selected subjects.' I didn't go. He isn't exactly the kind of speaker you break the door down to hear."

"Is there a description of the session?"

"Yeah. Let's see. A discussion on the consequences of mineralization of water supply in mood alteration. There is some stuff here about a study in England, a prison study, to reduce negative behavior in subjects by altering the mineral content of their water supply. It was a double-blind study, pretty good design from the description."

"Does the program list where he can be reached?"

"He's there with you, isn't he?"

"Humor me, Mark." Francis had used that expression with Mark for the last three years they had worked together. It was an anchor in their working relationship. Francis had often used the expression to ask Mark to go along with his eccentric ideas.

"Let's see, ah yes, no…it just says private consultant to the North American Water Cartel."

"Did you ever hear of that group before?" Francis asked.

"Never. You?"

"I'm afraid I may have been in their employment."

"So, they are a branch of the World Health Organization?"

"Yesterday, I would have said yes, but today, I'm not sure."

"Okay. Could we get back to what happened?" Mark asked.

"Sure, I came in to my lab tonight, flipped on the lights, and the room is empty. Everything is gone. This place is cleaned out like a duck with diarrhea."

"Everything? What about the Caduceus?"

"It's an empty lab, Mark. They even took the furniture."

"Wow, Francis. Hey, what can I do? What do you need from me?" Mark's voice now echoed his friendly tone of the past.

"I need you to sniff out this cartel. I need anything you can find about them. Plus, see if you can find out anything more about Lin, and Mark, why don't you contact Sanshi's family again and see if they've heard anything about him."

"Okay, give me a week or so, but what about you?" Mark asked. "Do you need some money or something?"

"I'm alright for now. I am here with Cassidy."

"The gal from Eureka Springs?"

"Yeah. She was here seeing a doctor, it's a long story. I have something amazing to tell you when I see you. I think the Caduceus works, but with some nasty side effects."

"Works? How?"

"The water revitalization may have cured her."

"Hell's bells, you were right."

"I can't be sure. There are a lot of intervening variables. I'll call you tomorrow."

"Sure, Francis. Take care."

Cassidy had listened to Francis' part of the conversation. "So, what does he know about Lin or the cartel?"

"Cassidy, can you believe, they sent him a letter from me, a letter with my signature, telling him I didn't think he was up to the project. Poor Mark, that must have really hurt him. He's a fine man, kind of sensitive for a scientist."

"What did he know about Lin? I heard you talking about him."

"He saw him at a conference a few years ago."

"What are you going to do now?"

"If you are up to it, I think we should go to the Senate."

"The Senate? In Washington?"

"That's where it was last time I looked." He quipped.

Chapter 26

Alford Purlough sat behind his desk. Outside his window he could see the outline of the White House. The door to his office opened unexpectedly. Doctor Lin came in.

Purlough was irritated by his presence. "Yes. What do you have to report?"

"The lab has been cleared out. The notes and results have been secured."

"Very good. Is there any possibility of the new location being discovered?"

"No. I have a secure site."

"Was Allenton any problem?"

"No. He was unaware of the impending move. We started as soon as he left the building yesterday and it was cleared in two hours. I made an independent decision."

"That's not what we paid you to do."

"I'm sure you will approve. I took the Caduceus."

"I thought your assessment of it was less than favorable."

"It is a useless relic. I decided, however, that it did represent evidence of the prior lab."

"I see. Yes, I can see your point."

"I will dispose of it discretely."

"Meaning what exactly?"

"It will never be seen again. I have a place to put it, out of the country, perhaps Paris."

"I want it destroyed. Cut it up with a torch and get rid of it."

"As you wish. It may, and I stress may, hold some promise in my hands."

"Promise?"

"Revitalization."

"That's not our focus, Doctor Lin. I don't want to waste any more time on it."

"As you wish. I'm certain Allenton was fabricating his results relative to its use."

"Did you review the findings on the mineralization project?"

"Everything is as we expected. The introduction of the soluble minerals below the level of detection does produce the desired effects of agitation and aggression."

"It seems my choice of Allenton was justified. He's a bright fellow. Do you think he suspected the true intention of the research?"

"No. He was blinded by his desire to use the Caduceus."

"Yes, he was emphatic about that device. Did you know he found a relic of the device in Greece that he used for the model?"

"Yes. I know this."

"I want the aggression formula in my office by tomorrow."

"No problem. I have personally brought you a report with the formula based on the results of the trials. Here, Mr. Purlough, I know how to meet deadlines."

"I want that water in the Senate and White House by the next regular shipment.

This is part of the larger plan. You are aware that the Cartel wants this in place before the vote for the war takes place?"

"We are on schedule, Mister Purlough."

"Are you absolutely confident that this new formulation will not alter the taste?"

"Soluble minerals have no taste at this level."

"There cannot be one suspicion that the water has been altered."

"Our testing lab has found no difference in taste. The effects are nearly immediate. The halls of Government will soon be filled with anger and aggression. Add to this, the issues following the nine-eleven attack, and we are assured the President will win approval to go to war. Not that the United States has ever had need of justification for going to war."

"Your indoctrination is showing, Doctor Lin."

"Yes, perhaps you are right. Is there anything else for the moment?"

"No, Doctor Lin, I'll be in touch. Your next assignment is in Africa. Return to the lab area and make certain nothing has been left behind."

"Yes, Mr. Purlough."

As soon as the door closed Alford pushed a button on his phone and speed dialed Compton. The phone rang only once.

"Yes?"

"Alford, here."

"Yes?"

"I have a full report for you. Can we talk uninterrupted?"

"Yes, go ahead."

"As of tonight, the lab has been relocated. Doctor Lin is now in charge. The preliminary results obtained by Allenton have confirmed the new formula. We will have this in the hands of our bottling people in two days. The altered water will be delivered with the next scheduled shipment."

"The new formula definitely promotes aggression?"

"Immediate changes in aggression."

"Have we begun to make progress in bringing the general public to doubt their municipal supplies?"

"Acid rain, arsenic pollution, ground water contamination, local, state and federal restrictions on water use are all moving forward."

"Good. And what about the push for the legislation?"

"We hope to have a bill introduced by our man this year. It may not get funding right away with all the money going towards the military and homeland security. The cogs are turning. We will get the legislation we want in time."

"We want a 21st Century Water Commission as soon as possible. The cartel can't continue to operate on our own funds at this level."

"We anticipate funding from seven to ten million in the first year after it is passed."

"How about the G8 membership?"

"The plan calls for appointments of people from both the public and private sector. My credentials have been arranged and I'm confident I will be appointed."

"You got yourself on the Boards we targeted?"

"It took some doing and some money, but I'm on the major boards. As I said, my credentials as a water policy specialist are in place."

"Good. Now, Alford, what about the other side of the aisle? Will it work to increase their aggression? We can't expect them all to vote for the war with the Republicans."

"The mood will be set by the time the vote comes to the floor. Everything is in place. I have been assured that we will get overwhelming approval. Later, when the war has officially begun and the infrastructure has been destroyed, we will begin supplying the water for the Armed Forces. Our military partners have assured us that one of the first targets to be destroyed is the water purification system in Iraq."

"Are we still forecasting a billion the first year?"

"That's the low side for the military contract. We will be building up local consumption all the while."

"That just leaves one problem, Alford."

"Yes, I know, you're still worried about Professor Allenton."

"If he catches wind of the real scope of the project – "

"After today, he is definitely relegated to the fringe element by his own eccentricity. The more he talks, the worse things will be for him. I really don't think we will have to take the next step with him."

"We have a lot of money on the table. We have removed people for a lot less than this investment."

"He was selected for his eccentric reputation. The people we have at his last lab will do the job of neutralizing him as a nut case. He's busy running around with a girl friend that has a terminal illness. He has just become unemployed and we made certain he couldn't go back to Columbia. He hasn't drawn a dime since we brought him here and there is no possible way to trace the lab back to the cartel. I am confident he will not be a problem for us. Lin may be more of a problem. His arrogance and loyalty to mother China keep cropping up."

"There's a lot of money and people on the line here, Alford. Twelve years of planning and bribes can be placed in jeopardy by anyone. If I hear of anything that has the slightest hint of a problem for the cartel, I am prepared to act. Drowning would be poetic justice, don't you think?"

"It will never come to that with Allenton." Alford said.

"Are we done with Lin?" Compton asked.

"Completely."

Chapter 27

Yan Lin had already made up his mind to keep the Caduceus. He made arrangements for it to be crated and sent to his home in Paris. He had considered destroying it, but something about it captured his attention. He wasn't certain if the enduring symbol carried with it magic properties, but growing up in China where the language utilizes enduring characters, he had come to deeply respect all symbols.

He stood in front of the device and touched the copper tubes as they wound their way down to a spigot. The design was primitive but elegant. The ferrite core had been cracked slightly as a result of the move. The battery supply had been haphazardly placed near the Caduceus by the workers. The copper wire leads were disconnected. The meteorite had been taken out of its holder on the top of the ferrite core and one of the tubes had broken at the seam that joined the smaller diameter tubes to the larger.

Lin approached the meteorite and held it in his hands. The dark molten mass had the quality of metal and crystal formed into rounded shapes on the ends. He found a ladder and placed the meteorite back into its copper holder. Then using some black electrical tape, he attempted to mend the connection in the tubes. Climbing down from the ladder, he connected the wire leads to the batteries.

When he stood in front of the Caduceus, Lin felt the hair on his head rise slightly. He thought the air around him was being charged.

"Curious!" he said aloud.

He pursed his lips together and moved his head slightly to the left and then to the right. He turned and began looking for the spring water that came with the device from the lab. He found a partially opened bottle with about a gallon of water remaining in it.

The crude holder for the jug had been damaged and could not be used. He placed a glass at the spigot and opened it. He climbed back to the top of the Caduceus and poured the water into the collecting bowls at the top. The water began to spiral through the tubes. A barely audible noise arose around him.

As he climbed down the ladder, Lin sensed an energy field around him. He opened the spigot and collected a large glass of water. As the water entered the glass it spun into spirals that seemed to spawn other spirals.

"Ridiculous!" he said aloud. Yet, he was compelled to drink. Perhaps it was the impulsive curiosity of a scientist who had confiscated someone else's work that made him put the glass to his lips. He drank deeply of the water and seeing a small quantity of the water remained, put the glass back to his lips and drained the last drops.

He sat the glass back below the spigot and sat back on a chair. He felt nothing.

"Magical water indeed!"

Rising from his chair, he decided to go out to dinner. As he walked outside to his parked car, a large figure stood in the shadow of the building.

"Give me your wallet!" a faceless man's voice demanded.

"Fuck you!" Lin yelled back.

"I'm not shitting you, pal. Hand over your wallet. I have a gun."

Lin felt no fear. Rage surged through his body. He lifted his hands above his head as if to strike the faceless figure that threatened him.

"Listen, you crazy fucker, I'm gonna kill your ass. Just hand over your wallet, and that watch."

Lin lunged at the man in the shadow. One shot rang out. Lin slumped to the sidewalk. He died angry.

Chapter 28

"What are you looking for?" Cassidy asked Francis. They had driven all night and then found a hotel room in Washington. Cassidy sat on the bed. She pushed pillows behind her and sat with her legs outstretched. Francis sat on an over-stuffed chair facing her.

"I'm pretty sure I know why you turned into a crazy woman." Francis replied. "It was the water I gave you."

"I knew it."

"I used some of the water that is usually shipped to the White House. That was supposed to be pure spring water. I was confident the supply would be pure, but I think it has been tampered with. It must have been enhanced to produce aggression. When I put the water through the Caduceus, it must have amplified the effect."

"Who would tamper with the bottled water that goes to the White House?"

"Those who who profit from war, or those who own and sell the bottled water to the Armed Forces. It definitely looks like we are going to war in the Mid East. The principal thing about war in the desert is the massive consumption of water."

"I don't understand. You think some group is manipulating the water supply of the White House?"

"Yes. The Senate and the White House are both supplied by the water that I ran through the Caduceus. Actually the Caduceus must have somehow concentrated the effects of the water. I was using manganese in my research to determine the effects it has on aggressive behavior. Your blood test came back with a high concentration of manganese. Now the results have been taken, the lab has been moved, and the Caduceus stolen. I have to conclude that something I found in the research satisfied those that funded the research. I may have been simply used to confirm a hypothesis or unwittingly develop a formula. Once I confirmed the aggressive effects of the water, the lab was no longer needed."

"Is that what you were doing? Were you trying to make people aggressive?"

"No. I was using a reverse process. You introduce a substance to the point of the negative effect and reduce the amount until you find the level at which the substance can be present but not cause the negative effect. I was also supposed to research healing water so it could be given to our Armed Forces if they were wounded or exposed to a toxic substance. The daily ingestion of water would inoculate them against infections."

"Did it work?"

"I only found the aggression factor. I produced a formula that would produce the aggression. The next step, had I been given the time, would have been to reduce the amount below the level that produced the unwanted behavior."

"What makes you think that aggression was the unwanted effect?"

"Well, what else makes sense? Cassidy, are you suggesting that I was working on the wanted effect? Someone actually wants to create aggression through bottled water?"

"Wouldn't you want soldiers to be aggressive?" Cassidy asked. "I mean it seems to me that if you want to have a war, you will want the men to be as aggressive as possible. If you want to prolong the war, then you would want the forces on the other side to be aggressive as well. It's like coaching football. I know something about this. I used to go out with a coach. His idea of a pre-game rally was to get the boys fired up as hell. The coach on the other side did the same thing. A good game comes from fired up athletes. I think that is why a lot of them looked the other way when the players started using steroids to pump up their performance. They want raw aggression. It sells."

"You have a point. Perhaps the desire all along was to manipulate the water supply to ensure support for war and once war has started, ensure the continuation of the war by making sure all sides are extremely aggressive."

"My Dad was in Vietnam and he always said war produced its own aggression. He never could settle down after the war. He turned to drugs and died a young man. Do you think they gave something to him?"

"What do you mean?"

"I'm just wondering if the Army gives men supplements in their food or water to make them mean. Remember that incident in My Lai, where the men went on a killing spree? Maybe they gave them something?"

"War is a savage business all on its own. You don't have to make men savage. War will do that for you."

"But what else makes sense, Francis? Remember in your lecture, the amazing increase in the use of bottled water. What if there is an attempt to make people more aggressive and manipulate the water supply. Isn't that something that the homeland security people are warning against? Haven't they said that the water supply in most towns is vulnerable?"

"You listened to my lecture."

"Shut up a minute. I think you might be right. What if there is a group that is causing people to have doubts about their water sources. At the same time they are manipulating local and state governments to put restrictions on water use. I went on vacation to Santa Fe, New Mexico, a year ago and the whole town was on some kind of water rationing system. The city government required a replacement of every toilet in town that used too much water. They would not approve outdoor watering unless it was on their schedule. I think this is happening all over the world. In Santa Fe people are discouraged from asking for tap water when eating out, but bottled water is easy to buy everywhere."

"The high desert areas have always had water shortages. But, it doesn't make sense for communities across the world to have turned to bottled water when their tap water is completely safe. There is a push toward bottled water despite increasing evidence that plastic bottles are causing major disposal problems."

"Didn't you say bottled water was becoming a billion dollar industry?"

"Yes."

"Wouldn't it be motive enough to supply the war zone? What kind of profits would come out of that?"

"Billions, I would say."

"How can you find out?"

"My idea was to look at the water in the Senate Building. Not the general water supply but the bottled water from Arkansas. If this is the same water I used in the Caduceus, then the water has had soluble minerals added below the taste threshold."

"Is that possible? Wouldn't you be able to taste it?"

"No. You didn't notice anything strange, did you, when you drank from the Caduceus?"

"No strange taste, but a warmth came over me, like at the hidden spring."

"You didn't say anything to me about a strange feeling."

"I thought it was sex. It had been so long since I had sex. I thought I had forgotten what it felt like inside me."

"What kind of warmth?"

"I don't know. It was a warm feeling that comes over you, almost like when you are embarrassed and your face goes all red."

"That was me. I am such a fantastic lover you got burned up with my love juice."

"Shut up. I don't get you sometimes. You are serious and then you become erotic."

"You're the one that brought up sex."

The heavy silence that characterized their relationship arose between them again.

"So, what are you going to do about it?" Cassidy asked.

"Sex?"

"No, well, maybe. I meant, what are you going to do about the water?"

"First, I'm going to have sex, hopefully, not alone. Then, let's get a good night sleep and go to the Senate Building in the morning. I'll start in the Clerk's office."

Sitting up in bed Cassidy let her top fall down. "Why don't you start right here?"

"Now who's being sexy?" Francis teased.

After they had made love, Francis went into the bathroom and she heard the shower running. Cassidy found the remote control and turned on the television. The news was on.

"Francis, Francis."

"Yes, my Sweet Baboo?" Francis stuck his head from behind the shower curtain.

"Come here. Hurry. What was the name of that man, the Chinese man?"

"Lin. Yan Lin. Why?"

"Get out here. He's on television."

Francis came out of the bathroom with a towel held in front of him. The news channel was showing a picture of Doctor Lin.

"Turn it up. Take it off mute," he yelled.

The news report was simple and direct. "Doctor Yan Lin, a scientist who had defected from China four years ago, was found dead earlier today outside a warehouse in the historical Georgetown commercial area. Police suspect a robbery. His wallet and other personal possessions were missing. Doctor Lin was employed by the National Water Cartel, a private group that promotes responsible water use. Doctor Lin is perhaps best known for his work on enzymes according to a spokesperson for the group, Alford Purlough. Mr. Purlough said tonight that Lin was a brilliant scientist and his contributions to the cause of water conservation will be greatly missed. This stands as another tragic reminder that crime goes unabated in our Nation's capital. Now, on to other news."

Cassidy switched off the television. Francis sat on the bed staring at her.

"I'm not entirely sure we are safe." Francis finally said.

Chapter 29

The floor of the Senate was crowded. A private school group in their navy plaid uniforms was on a tour to learn how the Senate conducts business. The tour was allowed to go onto the Senate Floor. Cassidy and Francis followed the group hoping to blend into the crowd as if they were chaperones. Most of the Senators had not taken their seats but were talking in small groups.

Stands holding large bottles of spring water were strategically placed around the floor of the Senate. The familiar logo of the Arkansas Spring Water Company was prominent on the outside of each up-turned bottle. As the group moved past the desks, Francis approached one of the ten gallon bottles and waited his turn. He discreetly poured his sample into a sterile beaker he had in his upper coat pocket.

He rejoined the tour group and noticed that the Senators were taking their seats. Visitors were asked to leave. Staying in line behind Cassidy, he continued to follow the tour group. They found seats at the back of the gallery and they listened as issues about the impending war in Iraq were debated. Senators on both sides of the aisle, even though they were most often in direct disagreement on issues, today displayed a uniformly angry mood.

One of the Senators rose to speak. He looked as if he could barely contain himself. His white hair contrasted with his red face as he spoke of the attacks of nine/eleven and shook his clenched fists in the air.

"Let's go." Francis whispered to Cassidy.

"Where?" she whispered.

"Let's try and find the place where Lin got killed."

"Are you crazy?"

"No. I think the Caduceus is there. If it is, the lab is there, too."

Cassidy's dark eyes shone brightly when she was excited.

The ride across town brought them to a police sub-station. They went inside. A police officer was at his desk behind a window. He looked up at them and nodded his head.

"May I help you?"

"Yes, sir. I was a friend of Doctor Lin, the man that was killed yesterday."

"I'm sorry about his death. It is an open file and currently under investigation. We really can't give out any information."

"It's not that, Officer. Some of his friends went together on a wreath. It has to do with his religion or something, to place a wreath where he actually died. I don't know how it all works. I'm a Presbyterian myself. So, anyway, I was wondering if you could just tell us where it happened."

"Well, I don't know – " The officer seemed a little put off by the request.

"Oh, please, sir." Cassidy spoke up. "I know his family. This is something I promised I would do for them. It has to do with his ability to make it to the other side and I told them I wouldn't let his immortal soul remain here in America."

"It's an old Chinese custom." Francis added. He adjusted his wire rim glasses as if to wipe a tear. "We're all pretty broke up about it."

"The exact area is marked off by a yellow police barrier. You couldn't cross that line," the officer said.

"Exactly. We don't want to disturb the investigation or anything. It's a small wreath. There are some symbols in Chinese on it." Francis said sincerely.

Cassidy had formed her hands as if in a prayerful stance. "It would mean so very much to the family."

"Well, I don't suppose it would do any harm. Yeah, what the hell."

After the officer gave Cassidy and Francis the address, they thanked him and returned to their car. Francis looked at Cassidy a long time.

"You fake it pretty good."

"I have my ways." She smugly smiled at him.

"Did you fake it with me?" Francis asked. A line of concern wrinkled his brow.

"No. You weren't dead. You realize the only adventures we have revolve around dead people. First there was Theodora, then I nearly bought it and now, Doctor Lin."

"Maybe it's you." Francis said. "I never ran into dead people before I met you."

"Like I said, I have my ways."

Francis smirked. In part, however, he was a bit anxious about their safety. If Lin had been killed by someone other than a robber, it might have been because he knew too much about the Cartel or had crossed them somehow. It was possible that it was simply a robbery that had gone bad, but Francis didn't like the feeling in the pit of his stomach.

The address was hard to find. It was in a run-down historical area where renovation had obviously not occurred. Some abandoned cars were parked on the streets. In one of the doorways, several thuggish-looking, young men hung out and shouted obscenities at women as they walked by. Francis parked as close as he could to the area where they could see the yellow police tape. To his relief a police car was parked nearby. A man in a suit was marking off another area and a second man was bent over picking up something.

"That's Lin's car." Francis said. "I saw it in New York the day we met."

The only building that seemed occupied was a squat-looking warehouse. With the police on the scene, the street in front of the warehouse seemed empty of troublemakers. The men inside the yellow tape didn't seem to notice them. Cassidy and Francis walked around to the side of the warehouse and tried to see inside. The windows had been sprayed with dark paint. A small window near a dumpster had been broken out. Francis stood on the dumpster while Cassidy looked around the corner to make sure the police were still busy.

"What do you see?" she yelled at him.

"It's here. I can see it. I think I can get the window open."

Francis reached inside and undid the latch. As he did he cut his forearm.

"Damn it."

"What?"

"I cut my arm."

"Good thing you're screwing a nurse. Let me see."

"No, not now. Stay there."

Francis pushed the window open and let himself down into the room. It was mostly dark, but with the light from the open window he could see enough to tell that the lab was partially set up. He approached the mineral testing equipment and quickly put together an analysis of the water sample he had retrieved from the Senate. The beaker turned color as he added the reactive agents.

He saw his Caduceus in the corner. He walked up to it and disconnected the batteries. The core had been broken and the area immediately around it had an odd smell like that of an over-heated electric appliance.

He went to a back door to let himself out, but the door had a double dead bolt on it. It took a key to get out or in. He turned around, took one more look at the Caduceus, and climbed out the window carefully using the dumpster again.

"What did you see?" Cassidy asked when he joined her at the corner of the building.

"It's there."

"The Caduceus?"

"Yes. It appears broken. Someone attempted to use it. The batteries were still hooked up. It has a shipping tag on it, to Paris."

"Did you test the water?"

"Yes."

"And?"

"Let's not talk here. I don't like the feeling this place gives me.

Francis and Cassidy walked quickly to the car and decided to return to their hotel room. As they drove Francis was quiet. Cassidy watched as his eyebrows arched up and down. She wondered if they always did that when he worked on a problem.

They continued to drive in silence for a few miles before Cassidy asked, "What are you going to do?"

"I'm not sure. The sample tested positive for high amounts of manganese."

"Is that the same stuff that made me go off the deep end?"

"Same stuff, but in a less concentrated form than you probably got. The Caduceus concentrated it, or at least I think it did."

"So, the water is fixed?"

"Buggered, if that is what you mean. I think I have to go to the Clerk's office and tell them. If someone is mineralizing the water they're using both at the Senate and the White House, someone should be told."

"Will they believe you?" Cassidy asked in earnest. The evidence was dubious at best, and without the Caduceus to show how the minerals could be concentrated, it was just a theory, a troubling theory, but still, just a theory.

"I'll just have to go and find out."

"I'm coming with you."

"No. I don't think that is a good idea. We need to split up for a few days. You need to go back to Joplin and get away from this town. I can't take the risk that something might happen to you, and if anything happens to me, no one will ever know why if you're not safe."

"You care!"

"Yes. I care."

That night the bed seemed too small to Cassidy as they both clung to the outsides. She found it difficult to lie there so close knowing their separation was just hours away. She had listened as Francis explained that he wanted her safely away from Washington. He had pointed out that it was already the murder capital of the United States. With their current situation, the odds were not good. If he were going to risk his reputation and possibly his life, he wanted to do it without putting her life in danger because of him. She wondered if they would ever see each other again. She worried if Francis would be safe, and if he got an audience, would they believe him.

Reluctantly, Cassidy was packed and ready for the cab that came for her at seven the next morning. They had agreed that she would get a flight back to Saint Louis and then a commuter flight to Joplin's small airport. The air hung heavy as she stood at the door of the cab.

"I never thanked you."

"For what?"

"For saving my life," she said.

"It's a beautiful life, inside a beautiful person. When this is over, I want us to spend time together, a lot of time."

"Without any dead people," she quipped, but regretted it almost instantly, "I'm sorry."

"No. You are right. We will have our moments together. I'm going to take you back to Eureka Springs when this is over. I promise."

"Promise me something else?"

"Yes. What?"

"See if you can find the real Sanshi. I'm afraid these people will do anything and he was such a sweet man. I tried to find him at home through Amnesty International, but I haven't heard anything yet. Have you talked to Mark?"

"I promise I'll continue to try to find Sanshi. I did call Mark and I'll let you know if he hears anything. When this is over, we will try together to find Sanshi and then you and I are going to get the Caduceus back under my control. "

When Cassidy was gone, Francis decided to let a cab take him to the Senate building. He was tired of fighting traffic and trying to park. As the cab pulled into traffic, he wished he'd been able to be more specific about when he'd see Cassidy again.

He waited for offices to open and then demanded and got a meeting with the Clerk. After an hour and a half of listening to Francis' story, the Clerk asked him to wait in a small office. It was nearly noon by the time a secretary came in to the room and asked him back to the Clerk's office.

Francis entered the room. The Clerk was at his desk and in a wing back chair a second figure faced the Clerk's desk. Francis could not see his face.

The Clerk rose and faced Francis.

"Doctor Allenton. I have consulted with several people concerning your story. We have done an investigation of our own and we are confident that the water supply is completely safe."

"You can't have the kind of equipment that would detect this level of soluble mineral." Francis protested.

"Doctor Allenton, we have every confidence this has been resolved. Our water policy consultant has come in and has had an independent lab in his organization run the test. Everything is as it should be."

The man stood and turned toward Francis. He extended his hand.

"Alford Purlough. Good to meet you, Doctor Allenton."

Chapter 30

"Doctor Allenton, Mister Purlough serves on a number of our committees." The Clerk said. "He has been filling me in on your reputation. Am I to understand, do I get this right, you believe that water is a living entity?"

"That's not exactly what I have said." Francis responded quickly.

"Alford has also told me you removed a priceless antiquity from the country of Greece. You are aware that this is contrary to international law. He tells me further that you believe you can construct some kind of healing water machine."

"It's based on an age old idea that has survived across time. I have already built it and it works." Francis again defended his life's work.

"You also believe that water has memory?" the Clerk continued.

"It's been proven."

"You also are reported to have said that water can be affected by thought control."

"Yes. I have reported that finding."

"And earlier, when you told me this fantastic story, didn't you say you were working for the World Health Organization?"

"Yes, sir." Francis could see the world spiraling against him.

"We have checked with them and their office in New York and they have no record of you as an employee."

"That is because I was working for Mister Purlough. He told me he was with the C.A.C." Francis gestured at Purlough.

"So now you want me to believe you are working for Mister Purlough. I'm sorry, Doctor Allenton. It is obvious that you have been under a lot of stress. I may have no choice here but to report you to the authorities. Making false accusations in the Senate is a national security problem."

"Nothing I have told you is false." Francis stood.

"Doctor Allenton. We thank you for your concern about the safety of the Senate. I am confident that our water supply is safe." The Clerk rose and went to the door and opened it. Two armed men came in. "These gentlemen will show you out."

Francis was led outside the building but allowed to walk away.

Back in the Senate building, the Clerk spoke first, "Alford, I told you he would be trouble."

"Let it go, John. He will not be any trouble. We have ruined his reputation, he is unemployed and totally without any support or credibility. The work of the Cartel is moving forward. Nothing, not even a wide-eyed crazy tale from the eccentric Doctor Allenton can stop us."

"I suppose you are right. I have already called the White House. He certainly won't get an audience there."

Epilogue

In 2003 the G8 Summit was held at Evian, France. The G8 Action Plan on Water begins, "As water is essential to life, lack of water can undermine human security. The international community should now redouble its efforts in this sector. Good governance needs to be promoted and capacity must be built for recipient countries to pursue an appropriate water policy, and financial resources should be properly directed to the water sector in a more efficient and effective way..."

How the G8 works: "The host country usually organizes several meetings in advance of the Summit, where personal representatives of the Leaders, known as 'Sherpas' (after the Himalayan porters who help others to climb mountain summits), come together to discuss potential agenda issues. Their discussions help Leaders focus attention on key subjects. The Sherpas, who often work as advisors in Leaders' offices, correspond directly with each other throughout the year concerning ongoing issues. After the Summit, they also oversee the implementation of Leaders' commitments made at the Summit. The Sherpas are supported by networks of other senior officials who focus on major economic, financial and political issues."

In April, 2005, the U.S. House passed a bill authorizing the Twenty First Century Water Commission Act. Members are to be hand-selected from private industry. Nine million dollars was appropriated

Private ventures are positioning to view water as a commodity and therefore, more and more open to commerce. Large amounts of water rights purchases are occurring. The idea of water as a basic human right is rebuffed.

Local, state and federal laws are increasingly regulating private water use.

Bottled water continues to be one of the few products consumed at a high level yet completely without regulation or control.

In 2005, Paris, France, launches a campaign to have its citizens return to drinking tap water.

Many soldiers in Iraq continue to be accused of brutal aggression against unarmed combatants and detainees. In March, 2005, The Army and Navy reveal that 26 prisoners have been killed while in the custody of U.S. forces in Iraq and Afghanistan. In all of the cases military investigators have concluded that the deaths were acts of criminal homicide.

The over-all mood in American government remains aggressive. New wars in Middle Eastern desert regions are contemplated.

Details of the Water Commission Act of 2005

This Act may be cited as the 'Twenty-First Century Water Commission Act of 2005'.

SEC. 2. FINDINGS.

Congress finds that –

(1) the Nation's water resources will be under increasing stress and pressure in the coming decades;

(2) a thorough assessment of technological and economic advances that can be employed to increase water supplies or otherwise meet water needs in every region of the country is important and long overdue; and

(3) a comprehensive strategy to increase water availability and ensure safe, adequate, reliable, and sustainable water supplies is vital to the economic and environmental future of the Nation.

SEC. 3. ESTABLISHMENT.

There is established a commission to be known as the 'Twenty-First Century Water Commission' (in this Act referred to as the 'Commission').

SEC. 4. DUTIES.

The duties of the Commission shall be to –

(1) use existing water assessments and conduct such additional assessments as may be necessary to project future water supply and demand;

(2) study current water management programs of Federal, Interstate, State, and local agencies, and private sector entities directed at increasing water supplies and improving the availability, reliability, and quality of freshwater resources; and

(3) consult with representatives of such agencies and entities to develop recommendations consistent with laws, treaties, decrees, and interstate compacts for a comprehensive water strategy which –

(A) respects the primary role of States in adjudicating, administering, and regulating water rights and water uses;

(B) identifies incentives intended to ensure an adequate and dependable supply of water to meet the needs of the United States for the next 50 years;

(C) suggests strategies that avoid increased mandates on State and local governments;

(D) eliminates duplication and conflict among Federal governmental programs;

(E) considers all available technologies and other methods to optimize water supply reliability, availability, and quality, while safeguarding the environment;

(F) recommends means of capturing excess water and flood water for conservation and use in the event of a drought;

(G) suggests financing options for comprehensive water management projects and for appropriate public works projects;

(H) suggests strategies to conserve existing water supplies, including recommendations for repairing aging infrastructure; and

(I) includes other objectives related to the effective management of the water supply to ensure reliability, availability, and quality, which the Commission shall consider appropriate.

SEC. 5. MEMBERSHIP.

(a) Number and Appointment – The Commission shall be composed of 9 members who shall be appointed not later than 90 days after the date of enactment of this Act. Member shall be appointed as follows:

(1) 5 members appointed by the President;

(2) 2 members appointed by the Speaker of the House of Representatives, in consultation with the Minority Leader of the House of Representatives; and

(3) 2 members appointed by the Majority Leader of the Senate, in consultation with the Minority Leader of the Senate.

(b) Qualifications – Members shall be appointed to the Commission from among individuals who –

(1) are of recognized standing and distinction in water policy issues; and including those who work on water issues at all levels of government and in the private sector . . . $9 million to be appropriated to carry out this act.

About the Author

Dennis Edwards received his PhD and Masters of Social Work from the
University of Illinois. He also earned a Masters in Leisure Studies and designed
and built playgrounds for children with disabilities. His formal career spanned
college administration, counseling, teaching, consulting and grant writing. He
also wrote a wide variety of newspaper and magazine articles as well as chapters
in textbooks in his chosen field of social work with a speciality in marriage
and family therapy. In addition to writing fiction, he is a poet, cartoonist, keen
observer of social trends and issues, and a weekly fly fisherman. Dennis has a
passionate commitment to nature especially in the Ozarks where he and his wife
live in concert with the wildlife on seven acres overlooking Table Rock Lake.
He is also a great-grandson of John Gray (1846-1910) who won seven Eisteddfod
chairs and was said to be the most prestigious Welsh poet in America.

About the Eureka Springs' setting:

The National Trust for Historic Preservation recently named Eureka Springs,
Arkansas, one of America's Distinctive Destinations for being one of the best
preserved and most unique communities in the United States. The spring water
in this area remains some of the purest in America. The 1886 Crescent Hotel
where Francis Allenton meets Cassidy Martin in *The Caduceus* is home to many
spirits including Theodora. The Crescent Hotel and Spa has undergone a multi-
million dollar restoration as has the downtown 1905 Basin Park Hotel.